the night has a thousand eyes

Also by Mandy Sayer

Fiction
Mood Indigo
Blind Luck
The Cross
Fifteen Kinds of Desire

Non-fiction
Dreamtime Alice
Velocity

Other
In the Gutter ... Looking at the Stars:
A Literary Adventure Through Kings Cross
(ed. with Louis Nowra)

the night has a thousand eyes

a novel

MANDY
SAYER

FOURTH ESTATE • *London, New York, Sydney* and *Auckland*

Fourth Estate
An imprint of HarperCollins*Publishers*

First published in Australia in 2007
by HarperCollins*Publishers* Australia Pty Limited
ABN 36 009 913 517
www.harpercollins.com.au

HarperCollins*Publishers*
25 Ryde Road, Pymble, Sydney, NSW 2073, Australia
31 View Road, Glenfield, Auckland 10, New Zealand
77–85 Fulham Palace Road, London, W6 8JB, United Kingdom
2 Bloor Street East, 20th floor, Toronto, Ontario M4W 1A8, Canada
10 East 53rd Street, New York NY 10022, USA

National Library of Australia Cataloguing-in-Publication data:

Sayer, Mandy.
    The night has a thousand eyes.
    ISBN 978 0 7322 8601 9 (hbk.).
    I. Title.
A823.3

Cover design by Gayna Murphy, Greendot Design
Author photo © Roslyn Sharp
Typeset in 11 on 17pt Baskerville BE Regular by Kirby Jones
Printed and bound in Australia by Griffin Press.

70gsm Bulky Book Ivory used by HarperCollins*Publishers* is a natural, recyclable
product made from wood grown in sustainable forests. The manufacturing processes
conform to the environmental regulations in the country of origin, Finland.

5 4 3 2 1   07 08 09 10

For Louis

1

One day, in June, it was so cold it didn't snow. Frozen peaches and plums hung from trees like Christmas decorations. I was out in the orchard, shooting pieces of fruit with my air gun. They were glistening with frost and icicles and, every time I hit one, they would shatter into a thousand glassy pieces. Our mother had been gone nearly two weeks and I was angry, not just at her but at the weather, at the holes in my Nikes, at my baby sister, who'd vomited on my sweatshirt during lunch. But most of all I was mad at Roy for driving our mother away again. My father just couldn't help himself when he came home from the pub. It would start off with a simple argument and then get louder and more crazy. Roy used to throw things at her: glasses of beer, ashtrays ... One night he even picked the cat up by the tail and swung her at Mum's head. Mum was OK, but Maxi died of a broken spine and we buried her under one of the apricot trees near the shed. To get back at him, my sister used to get me to piss into Roy's beer whenever he went to the toilet. All these things happened years ago, but it's that freezing day in June that's still with me, inside my headaches, my binges, my nightmares.

Mum had run away before, too many times to count. Sometimes, she'd try to take us kids with her, but Roy would always grab his gun and force us all back inside. After they'd had a big fight, she'd pack a bag and go and stay with her sister in Sydney. Either that or she'd check herself into Tenterfield Base Hospital. Once he broke her arm. Another time he cracked one of her ribs. But Mum never told the doctors the truth. She'd say she fell down some steps or crashed the car into a fence. Though she always came back after a week or two. *I couldn't leave my kids!* she'd cry, her arms opening out to us as she ran up the front stairs.

That day when I was shooting the frozen fruit, my sister Ruby was planting seeds at the edge of the orchard. Ruby was fourteen and thought she knew everything because Mum's sister – Aunty Candy – had once taken her to Surfers Paradise. But I could've told Ruby right then that she didn't know anything about growing marijuana. Well, you can't plant the seeds in frozen earth, for a start. Roy had the right equipment in the shed, the lights and chemicals. At night, the glow from the fluorescent bulbs lit up the windows and all you could see were two silvery rectangles in the darkness like a pair of staring eyes. There was a bed in one corner that he slept on some nights after he'd had a blue with Mum. He also kept porn magazines in there.

No one was allowed in Roy's shed, not me, not Ruby, not even Mum. I knew he also kept tools in there, and parts for his semitrailer. And one afternoon, when he forgot to close the door properly, I glimpsed a calendar from Tenterfield Automotive with a photo of a topless woman holding a large spanner between her breasts.

Son, he always said, *if I catch you snooping around my shed, I'll cut your balls off.*

Yeah, I always thought, *and I'll cut off your other leg.*

Of course, I wanted to snoop around his shed every chance I got. But the blinds were always drawn. He kept the door padlocked and the key on a ring attached to his wooden leg.

Roy'd had the accident a couple of years before. But I didn't know how it had happened because I'd been in foster care. When I was allowed to come back home, after twelve months, I found Roy with his right leg missing from the thigh down, and in its place was an old wooden prosthetic one that looked like it was about a hundred years old. His mates down the pub had already carved their names into it. Together with his red beard and bushy eyebrows, the wooden leg made him look like some drunken pirate. He never would tell me the real story of how he lost his limb, but nearly everyone in town had their own version of what went wrong.

On that cold and windy June day, the sky seemed closer to the ground, with clouds that looked like big, swollen bruises. I aimed and shot at another apricot, but missed. The slug ricocheted off a 44-gallon drum and I heard the sound of breaking glass. *Quit doing that,* said Ruby, not looking up from the ground. *You'll wake up Roy.*

I didn't pay attention to her because I was staring at the hole in one of the shed windows. I was too frightened to say anything. I knew Roy would whip me with his belt as punishment. I crept across the paddock, the frost crunching beneath my shoes, to get a closer look at the damage.

As I drew nearer, the hole in the pane got bigger, and I could see now that the curved cracks in the glass ran all the way to the wooden frame. There was a weird smell coming from inside, like wet dog fur. And then the stench of something worse, bad eggs maybe, or the hide of a possum that hadn't been tanned properly. I figured maybe it was the weed Roy was growing in there – all those strong chemicals. I pushed my hand through the hole and pulled the blind to one side. And what I saw in there still, after all these years, seems impossible and haunts me every day. There, lying face-up on the bed, was a body. Hands crossed over its chest and eyes closed, as if taking an afternoon nap. At first I thought it was one of those blow-up dolls I'd seen in Roy's magazines, the ones that have three vibrating holes. It was dressed in Ruby's red Kmart bustier, her miniskirt and high-heeled boots.

It was only when I squinted and peered closer that I recognised the familiar wispy black hair – flecked with grey – splayed across the pillow, the fleshy scar above her right eye, her hollow cheeks, which were now collapsing into her face. She was wearing her favourite red lipstick. As I gazed at her, I stopped breathing for a very long time and the next thing I knew I was yelling for Ruby. The orchard spun around me, like I was standing in the middle of an out-of-control carousel. Suddenly, my sister was at my side. She was shaking me and telling me to shut up. I wanted to piss and shit and collapse at the same time.

Ruby slapped me across the face. *Shut up, Mark. I mean it.* I glanced up at her and for a moment she suddenly seemed six inches taller.

Should we call the cops? I asked. I didn't dare look back inside the shed. The smell was putrid by now, and I was already imagining our mother rotting in there, along with Roy's possum skins.

Ruby began dragging me towards the house. It was the only place Mum and Roy could afford to rent after he'd lost his leg and then his truck-driving job. The grey weatherboard cottage was surrounded by weeds and brambles, rusting oil drums, spare truck parts, the shell of an old Holden station wagon. Roy never cleaned the junk away because we lived outside of town and didn't have any neighbours to complain about the mess.

Go and warm up the car, Ruby ordered, shoving me towards Roy's Fairlane parked in the drive. It was a red-and-white automatic from the '60s that he'd spent years and a fortune restoring. There was an old Kombi van beside it we sometimes used when we went camping. I didn't know what she was planning but I did as I was told. *Not the Fairlane!* she called after me. *The van! For fuck's sake, hurry up!*

I jumped in the driver's seat, throwing my air gun into the back. I turned on the ignition, revved and let the engine idle. It seemed like Ruby was taking a lifetime inside the house and I grew more and more scared. What if Roy woke up from his boozy stupor? What if he discovered what we knew? All of a sudden, I was cold all over and needed desperately to pee.

I left the van idling and ran up the back path, into the kitchen. There was no one there. I crept down the hall. I could hear snoring coming from Mum and Roy's bedroom, like some piece of rusting machinery. Roy had been passed out on the bed for an hour or so after coming home from the pub. I found Ruby in her room, whirling about, shoving clothes into an army surplus bag. The baby was asleep in her basket. *Grab some warm clothes, Mark*, Ruby hissed, not even looking at me. I stood there for a moment, holding my dick, which I always did when I was nervous. *For fuck's sake, hurry. He'll be awake soon.*

I went into my room and threw some clothes into my school backpack. I wondered what Ruby was planning for us. Maybe we were driving to the Tenterfield cop shop. I could hear her creeping down the hall. She paused outside my open door, holding the baby and a couple of bags. *Let's get going*, she breathed, before making for the kitchen. I grabbed my duffle coat and slung my backpack over my shoulder. I still needed to piss but I wanted to get out of that house before anything else went wrong. My Nikes squelched on the linoleum as I tiptoed down the hallway. Ruby was already outside in the yard. Through the screen door of the kitchen, I could see her long red hair blowing in the wind as she ran towards the van. The baby was mewling, like our old cat used to do at night when she was left outside in the cold. Thinking about the dead cat made me think about my mother and how we were leaving both Mum and Maxi behind forever, without taking any keepsakes or even saying a proper goodbye. And before I realised what I was doing – and I know this was a dumb thing – I was turning on my heel and creeping into Roy's bedroom.

He was lying face-up on the unmade bed, one arm tangled in the yellow chenille bedspread. His face was red and swollen and the room smelled of stale beer and cigarettes. His one-and-a-half legs were splayed into a V, or what would have been a V if he'd been wearing his prosthetic. The wooden limb was lying at the foot of the bed, next to an empty bottle of Carlton Cold.

I don't think anyone really plans to do this kind of thing – it just happens. It's like saying the wrong thing before you can stop yourself: you just can't predict how or when it will occur. And that's what happened to me that day.

I stepped over the sheets on the floor and picked up the leg. At first, I swung it back and forth in the air, testing the weight of it in my hand, as if it were a cricket bat or a tennis racquet. I could already see myself raising it above my shoulder and smashing it down on my father's head, killing him then and there, and I kept swinging it in slow arcs as I edged around the bed. But then I tripped on the sea-grass matting and bumped into the side table, knocking over the lamp, which crashed onto the floor, and suddenly my father was opening his eyes and lurching from the bed. Before I could pull away, he had me by the wrist and was yelling, *What the fuck's going on here?* As he pulled me down, I could see the bloodshot whites of his eyes. I tried to wriggle free but his grip was too tight. I thought of Ruby and the baby waiting in the van outside, about our mother, dressed in my sister's clothes, wasting away in the shed, and before I knew what I was doing I was slamming the leg against Roy's head.

He cried out and let go of my arm, yelling, *What the fuck? What the fuck?* I backed away from him, shocked by what I'd done. *You little cocksucker!* he cried. *I'll cut your balls off!* He lunged across the mattress, trying to grab his prosthetic, but I ducked away. I ran down the hall with it and out the door, my pack flapping against my shoulders. As I glanced back through the wire screen, I could see Roy crawling down the passage after me, his elbows like little crutches levering him across the lino, and all the while yelling he was going to kill me and the whole damn lot of us before the sun went down.

2

There've been a lot of rumours and gossip about how Roy Stamp lost his leg, but us blokes who worked with him at the trucking company know the real story. It had nothing to do with train tracks or gangrene: the accident happened one night when one of our truckies — Sparrow Turner — slipped him some LSD. It was obvious to everyone that Sparrow was going through a rough patch at the time, and we were all saying he was as nutty as a macadamia farm. He never got over the fact that his fiancée, Tanya, had dumped him a few months before and had taken up with Roy instead. Sparrow had been driving too much, doing five runs a week between Tenterfield and Walgett. He said he needed the extra money, but we all knew he was gutted by Tanya and Roy's affair and all he could do to keep sane was to stay on the road every night of the week.

As a teenager, Roy Stamp was someone you looked up to in this town. Whether he was playing football, or throwing a javelin, he didn't so much look like a pimply kid as a Nordic god, all muscles and sinew. He was the first boy at school to burn an Australian flag. Once, he put the hard word on a student teacher — he told us her name was Clare — and, what's more, she came across.

We used to watch him saunter down the main street every Sunday afternoon with his arm around a different girl. He came from an old dairy family who'd had land around here for more than a hundred years. Everyone knew that Roy Stamp was better than most of us and that one day he would move away from here and do something great with his life, or at least make a lot of money. If you'd told us twenty years ago that he'd wind up driving trucks with us, that he'd be unhappily married to Sapphire Tate, and that one night he'd end up on the Kamilaroi Highway with his right leg missing, we'd have told you that you were crazy and to stop talking shit.

The week he lost his leg — it was around New Year's Eve — he'd been delivering stone fruit. All of us at the company thought that was either a cruel irony or pretty hilarious, given how high he'd been when it happened. Peaches, apricots, plums — all from the orchards around here. He'd left town on a Friday afternoon. He only would've had, say, four hours' sleep. Some of us reckon he and Sapphire had had a big fight the night before — they weren't getting along — but no one can say for sure because they lived out past the Dinning farm and didn't have any close neighbours.

Like most of us long-haulers, Roy Stamp relied on a little assistance to keep him awake. The trip was over 500 k's, and he was due in at Walgett early that evening. We're not sure what he popped and how many, but our boss confirmed that Roy swung his truck into the drive of the Walgett warehouse at twenty past eight that night, crawled out of the cabin, covered in dust, and made a beeline for the RSL. He found Sparrow Turner hanging out there with five or six teenagers in the car park, drinking from a cask of wine. There was some teenage girl holding the plastic nozzle and pouring it straight into Sparrow's mouth.

The teenagers offered Roy a drink, which he accepted, but the real reason he stayed around in the company of Sparrow was the fact that the kids were also smoking pot, which Roy had a pretty big taste for. Not long after midnight, the old-timers began weaving out the side door of the club and into the car park, all on their way home. Soon Roy, Sparrow and the teenagers were in the back of a van, as the driver, some kid with a shaved head, careened out of the driveway and rubber-burned down the street.

They ended up in a paddock by the highway just out of town. About fifteen other kids were already there, huddled around a fire burning inside a 44-gallon drum. A girl strummed a guitar, someone was toasting marshmallows, another was chopping up a log with an axe and throwing the wood on the fire. It all seemed pretty harmless, like a high-school camping trip. Roy sat beside the girl playing the guitar and tried to sing along with her. Sparrow got a bit testy when he glimpsed Roy touching the hem of her dress.

Then Sparrow decided to offer Roy some tabs of acid. Roy grinned and pulled out a wad of cash, but Sparrow wouldn't take his money, and so Roy drank down two or three tabs with a plastic cup of cask wine. We've always known Roy was a little wild, but no one — not even Sparrow — had seen him want to wipe himself out with such determination.

At dawn, Roy was discovered lying unconscious by the highway, covered in blood. He'd lost his shoes. Flies and ants were crawling all over him. The axe was clamped in his right hand, like *he was some fallen warrior on a battlefield. But no one who worked at this company ever believed that Roy Stamp had tried to kill himself. No one but Sparrow, that is.*

We wouldn't have made it past the front gate if I hadn't stolen Roy's leg. I could still hear him cursing me from the house as I jumped into the van. Ruby was behind the wheel, squinting through the windscreen, as if the sun were shining directly in her eyes, even though it was now sinking and the sky was turning purple. The baby was sitting beside her, smiling, and pulling at her curly red hair. I took her into my arms and held her tight. Ruby hit the accelerator and we went skidding down the drive. I turned around and saw the screen door crash open and then Roy dragged himself out onto the veranda, howling after us, like some wounded animal. Ruby hunched over the wheel and swung the van onto the dirt track that led into town.

My sister was eighteen months older than I and was a much better driver. Roy had taught us both on the back roads, on weekend camping trips, but even then it was obvious after only a few lessons that Ruby had inherited his talent for doing donuts and burning rubber with the best of them. As soon as we'd be out of town on such trips, Roy would stop the van and let Ruby take over the wheel – the first time when she was only eleven. *Why can't you be more like your sister?* he used to say, while I sat in the back, writing my name onto the fogged window. I never really liked driving or camping, but Roy would always make me come along, so I could learn how to survive in the wild.

Even though I'd managed to steal Roy's prosthetic, I knew he still had a few old crutches lying around on the veranda, and that it was possible for him to drive his Fairlane automatic with only one leg. For this reason, I figured that he'd soon be on the road behind us, and that Ruby was driving us to the nearest police station – half-an-hour away and over the border – to report what had happened to our mother.

When I brought this up with Ruby, she flinched, like someone was giving her a needle or ripping off a band-aid.

Don't be stupid, Mark, she said. *When have those pigs ever helped us?*

I realised my hands were shaking so I clasped them tighter around the baby's stomach. She was right, of course. The police had always let us down. A few years before, when we'd still had a phone, we'd called the cops several times, whenever Roy went berserk and began smashing the place up. The one time they turned up at our door, it was hours later, and Roy had passed out in bed, looking as quiet and harmless as an old dog. *We don't like getting involved in domestics,* they said. *The women always change their minds.*

And then I thought of what would happen to us if the authorities did step in – we three kids would be split up permanently and shoved into a string of foster homes until each of us turned sixteen. There was no way I was going back into that kind of care – I wouldn't wish it on a pig.

Instead of taking the turnoff into town, Ruby slowed down and veered on to another, smaller, track that wound past the Dinning farm. Branches and twigs whipped the windscreen. The headlights shook as we jolted over potholes. I kept a firm grip on the baby. The silver bell on her bracelet kept tinkling like some faint, insistent doorbell.

The night suddenly seemed larger and darker, as if the entire world were just one big shadow that would eventually swallow us up. Clouds skidded beneath the half-moon. I couldn't stop thinking about my mother – her raven hair, the musky smell of her skin – as dead as a piece of roadkill and rotting in Roy's shed.

Stop blubbering, Mark! said Ruby. *I'm trying to think.*

But now that I'd started, I couldn't stop.

I mean it, Mark, she said, thumping me on the arm. The headlights flashed on a kangaroo as it leapt from the track into the bush.

Ruby, I asked, trying to make my voice sound normal. *What are we –*

Just keep a hold of the baby, she snapped. *Just see if you can do that.*

I fixed my eyes on the Dinning house. It was just a square of light on top of the hill, a faint wisp of smoke winding out of the chimney. It looked like something in a children's book, all warm and innocent. I wanted Ruby to hang a right and get us up there as quickly as possible, but I knew that would never happen because Ruby used to go to school with the Dinning girls and hated them. All three owned their own horses, which they eventually traded for late-model cars when their eighteenth birthdays came around.

The van lurched and shuddered as we drove past their house. I thought I could hear another car behind us, but, when I glanced back, I saw no headlights. I was desperate to ask Ruby what in the hell she had planned for us – or if she had any plan at all – but I knew if I did she'd thump me again. I wondered if she was going to contact one of our relations. Not that we had many to choose from. Of course, there was Roy's older brother, Bob, who lived in Glen Innes. But we'd only met him a couple of times because of some old family feud that went back years. Bob had married a woman called Margaret, but we had never met her. Roy had always said Bob was a bastard and that he'd cheated him out of his inheritance. But I knew, even then, that Roy said a lot of things, and most of them weren't true.

Our other relative was Mum's older sister, Candy, who lived in Sydney. We knew her a lot better because she'd come to visit a couple of times a year, whenever she needed to detox, and the time she got out of gaol. Roy used to call her a 'fucking freak'. But Ruby and I loved her because she always arrived with presents, and one time when Mum and Roy were having a fight, Candy rushed between them and punched Roy so hard in the face he was unconscious for over an hour. We didn't care that she'd been born a man and had her dick cut off when she was twenty-two. She was really funny and could put Roy in his place in a way that we'd never seen anyone else do before. She'd been born with a twin sister, named Laura, who was severely retarded and ended up in a special home.

If you ever need help, she'd say to me and Ruby, *you just call Aunty Candy*. She'd always mention this before she returned to the city, and, as I was sitting in the van clutching the baby, I wondered whether she'd always suspected something really bad would happen to us eventually, worse than Roy breaking Mum's arm or killing the cat.

Ruby, I said in a wavering voice, *how are we going to contact Candy?*

She didn't answer me for what seemed like a long time. We drove across a small bridge and up a rise. When we rounded the crest, I could see the lights from town shining like a cluster of stars. Ruby steered the van in behind some thick bushes, hit the brake, and we came to a stop.

We can track her down through Directory Assistance, she finally replied.

Of course, I hadn't thought of that. Ruby was always one step ahead of me.

The last time I'd tried to call Aunty Candy for help was a couple of years before, when Roy was threatening to put me in foster care. I was planning to run away and maybe live with her before he could make the final arrangements with the Department of Community Services. Roy was mad at me for all sorts of reasons, wagging school, accidentally setting the kitchen on fire ... He called me a pussy and said that maybe I should cut off my dick right now and become a queen like Candy. But mostly he was mad at me because, right after he'd finished restoring his Fairlane, I accidentally crashed it into a tree. When I finally found the right phone number and got hold of Candy's flatmate, Grant, to let them know I was running away to Sydney to live with them, Grant told me I'd be better off staying put: Candy had gone into rehab again and would probably remain there for months.

That was how I ended up living with the Ferguson family in Wee Waa for a whole year – because I'd crashed my father's car two days before my aunty had decided to get off junk again. The timing was completely wrong, and all that year I couldn't help dwelling on the fact that if I'd just crashed the Fairlane a few days earlier, or if Candy had been able to score some high-grade heroin that week, I wouldn't be stranded in an outback town, living in a small fibro house with a family of loonies, a family that wasn't so much interested in me as it was in the money they collected from DOCS to feed and clothe me, even though most of it went on their beer and cigarettes.

Ruby cut the motor and we sat in the darkness for a few moments. I couldn't see anything except the shadows of trees, not even the lights of the town. I could smell the baby's shitty nappy and feel her wriggling in my arms. She was the quietest kid anyone could hope to have. Everyone in town said so. Barely cried at all. The down side to that was she was fifteen months old and still hadn't uttered a single word, no Da-da, no Ma-ma. In fact, she wasn't even walking. Some mean people in town whispered between themselves that she was deaf and dumb or even autistic, but Mum always said it was because she had a pleasant nature and that she wouldn't begin to speak until she had something to say. She had large, deep green eyes and skin so translucent you could see all the veins in her arms and legs. No one could say she wasn't pretty.

Ruby flicked the inside light on and crawled into the back of the van. *Give her here,* she said, holding out her arms. I passed over the baby and then climbed into the back myself. I wanted to see what kind of camping stuff we had stored in there and if there was any food. Ruby undid the baby's jumpsuit and peeled off her soiled disposable nappy, screwing up her nose at the smell. *Get rid of this,* she said, palming it into my hand. I chucked it out the open window as far as I could while Ruby began rummaging through the built-in cabinets. She found an old washcloth, folded it into a triangle, laid the baby on top of it, and wrapped it around her waist and between her legs. We didn't have any safety pins so we stuck it together with gaffer tape.

It was freezing inside the van, so we huddled together under the blankets. The wind howled through the trees. The windows were framed with frost. I imagined Roy driving up and down the main street of town, scanning every figure and shadow, trying to track us down. He'd be circling the side streets, slowing here and there, whenever he saw a kid or a van. He'd be rubbing the stump of his leg, which he always did when he got mad. He said the nerves there twitched whenever his blood pressure shot up. And I knew, without asking Ruby, why we were now hiding in the bush. We'd have to wait until he gave up and drove home before we could sneak into town and make the call to Candy.

The hours passed slowly. Ruby sat chewing on a lock of her hair. The van smelled like dog's breath. I went through the cupboards and found some old cans of food. The labels had fallen off and I had to open three cans before I found something I could feed the baby. She gulped down the three-bean mix like there was nothing wrong at all, like she thought we were at home with Mum in front of the telly. Ruby wasn't hungry, so I ate a can of camp pie and saved the asparagus for another day.

I don't know what time it was when Ruby finally climbed back over into the driver's seat and started the engine. The baby and I had dozed off. But when I woke up, she was reversing the van out of the bush and on to the track. I went to crawl into the front with her.

Stay where you are, she said. *At least until we're out of town.* She was wearing one of Roy's old caps that had 'Walgett Trucking' embroidered on the front. The visor was pulled down hard over her face.

She drove slowly, as if we were trailing someone else, rather than possibly being followed. I held the baby close to me, listening to leaves and branches scratch the side of the van. Ruby turned on to the bitumen road and picked up speed. We swung right on to the highway that ran through town, and it was only then that I realised I hadn't peed for hours. I felt all sore and swollen inside. The overhead streetlights flashed like lightning through the windows of the van. I straightened up and peered outside. Through the windscreen, I could see the old weatherboard church, the brick post office, the Shell station closed for the night. The street was empty except for a mangy old dog that always foraged for food around Seth's Milk Bar. We passed the pub, and it was strange to see the car park without Roy's truck there; in fact, it was completely empty, something I couldn't remember ever seeing before.

I glimpsed a phone box at the end of the block, illuminated by a flickering light, and prayed that it was operating. Kids in our town – me and Ruby included – liked to break things just for the hell of it, like the tail-lights of parked cars, or the new fence at school. I guess we wanted to reduce anything that worked properly to being as useless as we always felt.

Suddenly, two headlights appeared further down the highway, like a pair of glaring eyes. Ruby hunched over the steering wheel and put her foot hard on the accelerator. We sped past the phone box and turned left down a side street. She pulled into a driveway and cut the motor and lights. It wasn't even twenty seconds before the vehicle raced past the corner and headed down the highway, moving so fast I couldn't tell if it was Roy's Fairlane or just some local farmer's old bomb. All I knew was that I'd stopped breathing.

I crawled over the front seat and opened the door. Ruby started to say something but I ignored her. I unzipped my jeans and peed against a white letterbox shaped like a chapel. It had a corny nativity scene beneath the slot – plastic Mary, Joseph, Baby Jesus, and a few winged angels. By the time I pulled up my zipper, my piss had frozen against them in a thousand icy stars.

Back on the highway, we headed south out of town. Ruby didn't even bother with the local telephone box. Maybe she already knew that it was out of order; maybe she'd even smashed it up herself. Or perhaps she realised she'd be too visible standing in its electric light. She kept her eyes nailed to the white lines on the road and in the next half an hour we saw no other cars – just two semitrailers heading in the opposite direction, speeding so fast the truckies wouldn't have had time to see that it was a fourteen-year-old girl driving past them in a van.

It was near dawn when we crossed the border into New South Wales and reached Tenterfield, a town of old pubs and wide streets. We followed the winding road. Again, we saw no one – the place looked as if it had been evacuated. I pointed to a phone box outside a bank. *There*, I said, *let's call her now.* But Ruby just shook her head and kept on driving. *It's five in the morning,* she replied. *Do you think she's gunna pick up the phone now?*

Of course, she was right again. Even if we got Candy's answering machine, it wasn't like we could leave a number for her to return our call. Candy never got up before eleven o'clock, and even later in winter.

We parked by a stream at the edge of town. The sun was rising and the pastures were shining with bluish frost. The baby was asleep between two pillows, her thumb in her mouth, content as a puppy. For a moment, I envied her serenity, her absolute trust in the world. Ruby crawled into the back with me and it was only after she'd pulled off

Roy's cap that I saw the toll the night had taken on her. In the half-light, her skin looked sepia toned, as if all the blood had been drained from her body. The two squint lines between her eyebrows now seemed deep and permanent, making her look years older, like our mother. I realised then that most of her bravado was just an act, and that deep down she was just as frightened and confused as I was. She slipped under the blanket and closed her eyes. Within five minutes, she was quietly snoring.

While Ruby and the baby slept, I grabbed my air gun and climbed out of the van. After all the panic of the night before, I was edgy and restless. The smell of baby shit and mould in the back of the van was suffocating and I had to escape and stretch my legs.

I followed the stream for a while, aiming my gun at crows, galahs, even one or two possums. Cows stared at me as if I'd done something wrong, as if I'd managed to offend them. I'd never actually shot a live animal before and wasn't about to start now. My only targets had been rusty tin cans, bottles, and the stone fruit that froze on our trees back home. Roy used to make fun of me for being such a wuss, but I just didn't like the thought of taking a life. Of course, I was deliberately setting myself apart from my father. I didn't want to grow up like him.

The eucalypts were webbed with rust-coloured mistletoe that glistened with morning dew. The trees lined the banks of the stream, as if they were guarding it. I realised I was hungry again and wished I could find a plum or apricot tree.

In my pocket, I had a packet of chewing gum and exactly four dollars and fifty-five cents.

The stream led me to some shops on the south side of town. It would have been about seven o'clock by then because I passed a pub that was already opening and a man was chalking counter-lunch specials on a blackboard out the front. The words 'rissoles' and 'sausages' made my stomach grumble. The man paused and glanced up at me and my air gun. He suddenly raised his hands. *Don't shoot!* he said, laughing at his own joke.

On the next block, I found a truck stop and convenience store. My plan was pretty simple: I would buy something really cheap, say, a packet of chips, but I would hang around a bit longer after my purchase and steal a couple of other things – some more food and maybe some nappies for the baby. I'd done this kind of thing before, back in our own town – it all had to do with the timing. The extra food would keep us going until Ruby and I could contact Candy and plan our next move.

I left the air gun behind some garbage bins out the front. I didn't want to alarm anyone and, besides, I needed my hands free. The shop assistant was a bored teenage girl who was eating Twisties and watching a cartoon on a portable television. She barely looked at me as I paid for my corn chips. In fact, she seemed annoyed that I'd interrupted *The Bugs Bunny Show* and I was left to wander freely down the aisles and fill my pockets with peanuts and chocolates. A packet of disposable nappies went under my coat, and, by the time I was out the door, I felt all lumpy and shapeless, as if I'd suddenly gained five kilos.

I picked up my gun and experienced a sense of relief as I walked down the street. I couldn't wait to get back to the van to tell Ruby what I'd done. She'd be impressed that I'd thought of the nappies. I wedged the gun between my elbow and ribs, tore open a packet of peanuts, and began wolfing them down, but, the more I ate, the hungrier I felt. As I neared the pub, I was scrabbling inside the foil packet, scooping up the last of the nuts, and, when I looked up, what I saw seemed like an apparition.

With the aid of his crutches, my father was hobbling away from his Fairlane and heading towards the pub, his eyes fixed on the open door. A bloodied piece of material was pasted to the side of his head, where I'd bashed him. He looked sad, pathetic, and I almost felt sorry for him. His red hair was wet and straggly and I could see he didn't have his false teeth in. And, before I could duck or run the other way, he saw me standing there, holding my empty packet of peanuts.

You little cunt! he yelled, swinging himself towards me. *You're just like your mother. I'll fuckin' get you next.*

3

We all knew when we were trying to teach him trigonometry and English verse that he was headed for a life of trouble. During Roy's years here, he was a handful, all right, and his kids, Ruby and Mark, turned out to be not much better. As a boy, he'd write rude messages on the blackboard, or put spiders in our purses. Once he exposed himself to a young teacher – Clare Wilcott – and encouraged her to do the same to him. That disaster ended up in Children's Court and the teacher resigned from the Education Department.

Another time we discovered our Australian flag reduced to ashes and empty liquor bottles in the change room, and we all, of course, knew who'd been behind it. So unlike his older brother, Robert, who was always nice and polite. Robert went on to create a successful business for himself in Glen Innes and still sends us handmade Christmas cards every year. We pin them up on the noticeboard in the staff tearoom.

The brothers weren't close, but from time to time Robert would lend Roy money. And it was Robert who explained to us the truth about the accident. He'd heard that people in town were gossiping about Roy and he rang us to explain what really had happened.

He told us that Roy had been seeing this woman for only about a fortnight or so. It was New Year's Eve and he was just finishing up a long-haul run from Walgett. On his way home, he stopped off in Tenterfield, where she lived. Of course, she was much younger than him. Her name was Halo. We remember her well: she excelled in art — pottery, mostly — but failed almost every other subject and dropped out of school when she was sixteeen. Rumour had it that she came from a rotten family, that her mother was into drugs. Anyway, that New Year's Eve, Roy took her out to a local disco, where they drank and danced for most of the night. Halo was a big ABBA fan.

The management had arranged for a series of smoke bombs to go off on the dance floor at the stroke of midnight. It was the height of summer, and stinking hot. By eleven pm the air-conditioning system had broken down and people were pouring water down each other's backs. Roy and Halo were dancing to the Bee Gees. Someone later said the song was 'Stayin' Alive'. As more and more people danced, the temperature rose. Roy was spinning about, close to the stage, when, due to the heat, one of the smoke bombs exploded, and then it set off the others in an instant chain reaction. Roy was hit by a wave of shrapnel that blew him clear across the nightclub. His ear drums exploded. They were able to save his eyesight and left arm but his right leg was so badly damaged it had to be amputated the following day. We don't know what happened to Halo — no one seems to know.

Robert told us this in confidence. He'd known us most of his *life and knew he could trust us. And even though we didn't condone Roy's shocking behaviour, we all agreed that no man deserves to lose his leg for having an extramarital fling.*

For a moment I was too stunned to move. My hand seemed frozen inside the empty packet of peanuts. Roy was heading towards me, crutches swinging as he levered himself along the footpath. All the time he was yelling, *Bastard! Cunt! Arsehole!* It seemed impossible that he could have found us, and I wondered if he'd been tipped off by someone or that it was just a cruel accident that our paths had crossed like this so far from home. *I know what youse two are up to!* His face was tight and flushed, as if he'd been drinking all night. *Cops won't believe ya.* He was almost upon me by then, about ten metres away, and what happened next unfolded like a scene in slow motion, like something in one of those action films. I dropped the foil packet and, before I knew what I was doing, I was raising my air gun and aiming right at him. *You fuck! You puny little fuck!* That was the last thing he said before I pulled the trigger and shot him in the eye. He went down backwards, arms swimming in the air. His head hitting concrete sounded like a door slamming.

I didn't waste any more time. Faces were already appearing in windows, no doubt wondering what Roy was yelling about. I ran past the pub and made for the stream that would lead me back to the van. I ran as if a tidal wave were about to crush me. Trees flew past me in a blur; a flock of birds scattered into the sky. My heart was drumming loudly; I could feel the blood beating inside my ears. I rounded a clump of bushes and only began to slow down when the mud-caked van was within sight.

I opened the door on the driver's side, and chucked my air gun and the nappies on the passenger seat. I started the ignition, put the gear into first and hit the accelerator. *What the fuck are you doing?* I heard Ruby yell from the back. *Your driving's hopeless!* She was now clambering between the front seats. She punched my arm and tried to wrestle the wheel from me but I felt so panicky I couldn't let go. The ground was wet and the van slithered in crazy S's across the paddock, towards the dirt track up ahead. My right foot seemed welded to the pedal and I was gripped by the certainty that Roy was right behind us in his Fairlane, ready to gun us down. The baby was crying. Ruby was screaming. The van jolted over potholes and rocks, and before I could swerve, a huge, jagged boulder was rushing towards us. We hit it hard and suddenly were airborne, like we were on some ride at a fairground. I could see the branches of trees passing, and a big blue rectangle of sky framed by the van's windscreen. But then we took a nosedive and I was horrified to see three or four frightened calves in our path. I pulled the steering wheel into a hard left in the opposite direction. We hit the ground and I kept swinging left, trying to miss the last calf, when a tree jumped up before us and we crashed.

Everything went quiet. Dust hung in the air amidst falling leaves; a frill of blood coloured the windscreen. I touched my brow and felt where I'd hit my head on the steering wheel. It was already sore and throbbing.

Fuck, Mark, cried Ruby, rubbing her shoulder. *You wanna get us killed?*

And then I thought of the baby: that she was still in the back, that she was so quiet and awfully still. Ruby must have thought the same thing because we both turned and scrambled over the seats. At first, she didn't seem to be anywhere – all I could see were clothes strewn all over the place. It was Ruby who found her, bundled in an overcoat, wedged right up against the passenger seat. She had a small abrasion on her cheek, which looked like it would bruise, but apart from that she seemed unharmed. Then she waved one fist in the air, as if she were celebrating her own survival.

Ruby started swearing at me again, paying me out. *You idiot, idiot fuck!* When she talked like that, she reminded me of Roy, mean and filthy as guts. She finally took a breath and that's when I told her.

I saw Roy. Back in town.

She tensed and ran a hand through her hair.

He was on his crutches, going into the pub.

She blinked and fixed me with a hard stare.

He saw me coming out of the store. Said he was going to kill us all.

She took a deep breath and peered out the window. *If this is some kind of joke –*

I did, Ruby. I swear on my mother's – I chewed on the insides of my cheeks and swallowed hard. *I shot him in the eye with my air gun.*

I thought Ruby would panic, as I had, but her expression remained tight and serious, like she was trying to solve some complicated maths problem in her head. She put the baby on the mattress, climbed over the seat, and opened the passenger door. I followed, and we walked around the van, inspecting the damage. Fortunately, we'd crashed front-on, and the bull bar had taken the brunt of the impact. The bonnet was dented and the right headlight was cracked, but, apart from that, there didn't seem to be too much damage. As she fingered the headlight, Ruby's shoulders were still hunched but she seemed to have calmed down a little. *We'll have to stay off the main roads,* she murmured. And then, almost as an afterthought, she said to me quietly, *Don't ever do that again. You know you can't drive.*

I held the baby in my arms as Ruby started the ignition and threw the van into reverse. Luckily, it was still running well, in spite of the crash. I felt dumb and kind of ashamed of myself that I'd been unable to look after my sisters better, that I'd botched our escape. I guess it was the shock of seeing Roy so close and unexpectedly and not having the time to think properly. Ruby was silent as she steered us on to the dirt road that wound further away from Tenterfield. It rose up a steep incline into a cattle pasture. The clouds were low. As the grazing cows backed off the track to let us pass, their eyes looked large and haunted, as if they had glimpsed our father shadowing us in the distance and could foresee what would happen next.

Ruby steered us on to an even narrower trail between two barbed-wire fences. A mud-coloured creek ran beside it, clotted with the rusting bodies of abandoned cars. It was a good feeling to be putting more distance between ourselves and Roy but I also sensed we were getting further away from a public telephone box and that important call to our aunt in Sydney. The baby started wriggling in my arms and I suddenly remembered that I had packets of chocolates and chips in my pockets. I took out the chips and tossed them onto Ruby's lap. She glanced at them, surprised.

Lifted 'em, I said proudly. *And a packet of Huggies, too.* It was the first time I had seen her smile in a long time – days, weeks even. She ripped the packet open with her teeth and started eating with her left hand, while I fed the baby a fruit bar and some chocolate. It seemed as if I'd been forgiven for crashing the van and some of the panic I felt earlier was beginning to drain away.

Did he try to chase you? she asked, as she steered us left on to a narrow bitumen road.

Not after I shot him, I boasted. *You should've seen him. Fell over backwards like a sack of shit – right in the middle of the main street!*

And then she surprised me: in spite of herself, she began laughing and thumping the steering wheel with the heel of her hand. And that of course made me laugh, too, even though I wasn't happy, and the sound of us chortling excited the baby, and she began clapping her hands and rubbing melted chocolate on to her face.

Once we calmed down, Ruby's brow furrowed and she grew serious again. *'Course that won't slow him down forever. Did he see which direction you headed?*

I wiped the baby's mouth with the sleeve of my jacket. *Hard to say. Hit his head on the concrete. When I was running along the stream, I couldn't see him behind me.*

Ruby pursed her lips. I could tell what she was thinking. *Probably reckons we're headed for Glen Innes. Uncle Bob's place.*

We can't go there, I said.

Ruby rolled her eyes. *Der, Sherlock. It's the first place he'll look. If he can still drive, he'll be heading down the New England Highway. We'll have to steer clear of it.* She began chewing her bottom lip.

Up ahead, the bitumen road ended at a small wooden cattle bridge. On the other side was a dirt trail dotted with cows. *I hate having to do this*, said Ruby, throwing the gear back into first. She fixed her eyes on the bridge. *Just hold tight to the baby.*

For the next few hours, we followed a logging track that wound through deep, purple ranges into a national park. Ruby had to concentrate so much I didn't dare speak, in case I distracted her. The track was narrow and gravelly, with barely enough room for two-way traffic. There were hairpin turns, sharp corners, and, on the passenger side, the trail fell away into drops so steep that when we veered to the edge my stomach would flip and I had to close my eyes. Every now and then, a kangaroo leapt in front of the van and bounded off into the scrub. When the curves were totally blind, Ruby thumped the horn to warn any oncoming traffic, but she needn't have bothered because we passed no other vehicles.

Clouds were clustering above the mountain peaks and the sky looked bleak and grey. I thought about how, at this very time yesterday, I'd been eating Coco Pops in front of the telly with my feet resting on the top of the heater. I'd been watching a repeat of *Australia's Funniest Home Videos* and thinking they weren't that funny. Yet, what I would have given to have been able to reverse time and be back there again, back when I thought my mother was still alive.

We descended the mountain in a kind of corkscrew motion and the cow pastures were overtaken by trees and bush. Every now and then there was a flash of colour between branches and I saw cockatoos and galahs fanning skyward. The steep gradient of the track plateaued out about three-quarters of the way down, where a ravine meandered between reeds and rocks. On either side of the bank were rows of greying tree trunks between discarded logs and branches. Everything looked dead and desolate. It felt like a cemetery.

Should we rest here? Ruby asked. It was the first thing she'd said to me in over two hours. Even though she looked weary, I shook my head. The area felt too creepy to camp in, but I didn't say this. All I said was, *If a car passes, they'll be sure to see us from the track.* Ruby nodded carefully, as if she hadn't thought of that.

But we should stop soon, I added. *The baby's starting to stink again.*

Ruby sighed and changed gears, muttering, *All she does is eat and shit.*

After about half an hour, we finally reached the valley and crossed a bridge over a wide, shallow stream.

I'm buggered, Mark, said Ruby. Once we reached the opposite side, she turned left, drove about twenty metres, and stopped. A group of cows backed off and stared at us from a distance. *At least there's fresh water*, she said. *We can all have a bath.*

I looked out the window and saw more rotting stumps and discarded logs along the bank. Large rocks rose out of the stream like volcanic islands in a sea. I didn't like the feel of this place, but I didn't say anything. Ruby had exhausted herself getting us this far away from Roy and I knew better than to complain. I didn't really know where we were headed but, glancing at the odometer, I realised we'd already travelled many k's that day.

Put up the tarp, she said, taking the baby from me. *We'll stay here till tomorrow.*

You sure that's a good idea? I asked. *Anyone can see us from the road.* That was rule number one Roy had taught us about illegal camping – make sure you're not visible to passing cars. This was just an excuse, of course: I just didn't want to stay in that cold, grey valley. It was so isolated it felt dangerous. If we cried for help, only the birds would hear.

I can't drive any more, Ruby said. *I'm rooted.*

She climbed into the back of the van to change the baby's nappy while I began collecting firewood. The sky darkened and it started to rain lightly, so I pushed the branches and logs under the van to keep them dry.

I hated putting up the tarp on my own – I could never get the poles straight. I tied one corner of it to the top of the van, and another corner to a tree. The ground must have been softened by rain because, when it came to hammering in the stakes, it was surprisingly easy, and soon the tarp stood tall and straight, even better than Ruby could have done.

I was just starting to feel pleased with myself when I heard a noise in the distance – the sound of an engine. I stood still and listened hard. It was coming from the north, from the track we'd just been on. I scoured the mountainside for a glimpse of some kind of vehicle but could see nothing except rocks and trees. I hid behind the van, holding my breath as the noise grew louder and closer. I was just about to call Ruby and tell her to start the van when I saw a motorbike swerve around a bend. As the bike hit the bridge, I was relieved to see the motorcyclist had two legs and was wearing overalls. He seemed harmless enough. But, about halfway across the bridge, he slowed down a little, craned his head, and glared at our campsite. I began to feel panicky again. Maybe Roy had paid him to hunt us down. The bike slowed to a crawl. The man kept staring. He was about Roy's age and wasn't wearing a helmet. I raised my arm, ready to bang on the door of the van to warn Ruby, when the man continued along the bridge and accelerated up the track and into the next set of ranges.

I was glad that he was gone, but still felt jittery. I busied myself by making a little pyramid of branches, twigs and leaves under one corner of the tarp. I found a cigarette lighter in the glove compartment of the van. It took a few attempts and I burned my fingertips several times. Eventually, some tiny flames caught on. When I blew lightly, they began to flare.

While Ruby and the baby dozed, I opened some cans and heated them on the fire. Baked beans, pea and ham soup, spaghetti. I fetched fresh water in an empty four-litre plastic container we always kept stowed under the front seat. The stream was freezing, but I waded out into it and splashed my face. It made me feel alert again. I sat by the fire and gulped down the beans, then I washed the fork, rinsed the can out, filled it with water and stuck it back into the fire. I knew there was instant coffee in the van and that, when she woke up, it would make Ruby happy to be able to drink a cup.

It was around this time that I heard the sound of the motorbike again. At first it was just a purr in the distance – way up in the ranges – but, after a few minutes, I had to admit to myself that it was growing louder and heading back in our direction. It grew into a rumble and soon the same bike was rounding a curve and heading back towards the stream. Perhaps he was a cattle farmer, or maybe he was just plain lost. The bike slowed down again, and I found myself praying that he would cross the bridge and disappear from our lives forever.

But instead, he swerved off the track and came to a stop by the bank of the stream. I banged on the side of the van. *Ruby*, I cried, *wake up.*

The curtains parted and her face appeared at one of the windows, all creased and full of sleep. I could see the man marching straight towards us. Ruby must have seen my fear because she was out the back door with the baby in seconds. The man's grey hair was wet and plastered against his scalp. He had a mean expression on his face, like maybe we'd stolen something from him.

Private property! he barked, stopping a few metres before us. His lips were so thin that he didn't seem to have a proper mouth, just something like a slit in a letterbox. He cast his eyes over the campsite. *Where's your parents?*

Ruby and I glanced at each other. *Bush walking,* she said.

You know youse aren't allowed to camp here?

Ruby and I stared at him blankly. *We're not camping,* she said.

The man eyed the fire and the wood I'd collected.

We're just warming up some lunch, she added apologetically. And then, for extra effect, I said, *The baby has to eat every four hours.* And, right on cue, as if she sensed that we were in trouble, the baby began to whine a little and kick her feet.

The man's eyes narrowed. He looked at the fire, with the three cans balanced on it, and back at the baby.

All right, he said. *But you tell your parents to clean up before youse leave. I'm tired of garbage being left on my property.*

OK, I said.

We'll tell them, said Ruby.

He nodded curtly. *Better feed the ankle-biter before it scares all my cattle away.*

He walked back to his motorbike, straddled it, then sped off over the bridge and up the logging track.

Well, said Ruby happily. *We showed him.*

I shook my head. *He'll be back.*

Ruby passed me the baby. *I'm starving.* She crouched beside the fire and used her coat sleeve as a pot holder to lift off the can of spaghetti.

I mean it, Ruby. He'll be back to check on us.

She ignored me and began eating the spaghetti and staring at the stream, as if the water could give her advice about what we should do next. I sat with the baby and fed her spoonfuls of pea and ham soup, which she lapped up hungrily. It was still lightly raining. On the opposite bank, cows huddled beneath a willow tree. I began to wonder about the one thing that could have made me happy that afternoon, a place we could visit that would wash away some of the shock and bad times of these past few days.

If he comes back and finds us still camped here and with no parents around, I said, *he's sure to raise the alarm.*

Ruby scraped the bottom of the can. *I know that, dummy.*

Where does that track lead? I asked, motioning to the logging trail that wound from the bridge up into the next set of ranges.

Through the mountains. It connects up with the highway. From there, it goes to Casino.

This was good news to me but I struggled to stay calm, pretending not to care where we were headed. *Casino,* I said. *That's only an hour from the coast.*

Don't tell me – started Ruby, a sarcastic edge to her voice. *It's all right for you. You've already been there.*

She wiped her mouth with the back of her hand. *It's*

not that special. Just waves and bluebottles and wet sand in your pants.

I really want to, Ruby. It'll be warmer, too.

She shrugged. *When we get to Casino tomorrow, we'll call Candy.*

Tomorrow?

Can't drive the highway in the day, said Ruby. *Everyone'll see us.*

I shrugged, as if I didn't care, but of course I hadn't thought that far ahead. All I could think of was swimming in the ocean instead of wading in that smelly water hole near our house that was full of croaking frogs.

Get the tarp down, Mark. I'm going to have a coffee.

I was glad we'd be leaving that dark, rainy valley, but it annoyed me that I was the one who had to pack the camp away so soon after she'd ordered me to set it up.

Half an hour later we were back on the logging track. The sleep and food must have done Ruby some good, because she hummed to herself as she hunched over the steering wheel. It was slow-going though, with so many curves and steep inclines. I could tell she didn't want to discuss the coast any more. I also knew that the more I tried to persuade her to drive to the beach, the less inclined she'd be to agree with me. In that way, she was like Roy. Mum used to call her 'contrary', but I always thought that that was just a nice way of saying she could be a bit of a bitch at times.

We didn't talk at all as we wound through the ranges. The baby dozed in my arms. Kangaroos gazed down at us from rocks and ledges before leaping off into the bush. Sometimes we passed a farmhouse or barn, but mostly we just saw herds of cattle and domestic horses. There were also a couple of derelict cottages overgrown with weeds and flowering creepers. After about an hour or so, the world flattened out and began to grow lush and green. The track ran alongside a river and I liked watching the rain dimple the surface of the water. The bank was lined with trees taller than telegraph poles, and the branches were webbed with thick, looping vines. When the track ran through into a new property, there was always a sign saying 'No camping allowed' but occasionally I spotted a tent set up way back from the track, almost hidden in the thick rainforest. One sign said 'No camping aloud', and I made a joke to Ruby that we could set up our tent right here on this farm as long as we did it quietly.

Suddenly, Ruby thought she saw a horse running through the forest and slowed down. When the creature charged out in front of us, she hit the brakes. I was startled to see a large camel standing only metres from the van. He was looking directly at us through the windscreen and, when I peered closer, I could see that he was pissing on the trail. His fur was grey and mangy, but there were bald patches over his hump. Even the baby was fascinated as she peered over the dashboard.

Probably feral, murmured Ruby. *Escaped from a circus.*

And that's when she glimpsed the gauge to her left and realised the big mistake we'd made: the arrow had slipped to EMPTY. We hadn't thought to check it earlier and we were at least two hours' drive away from the nearest petrol station.

We stared at the camel as he continued to piss. It was still raining and for a moment the sun peeked out between the clouds and the light made its wet fur glisten. I knew Ruby was cursing herself for not realising sooner that we would eventually run out of petrol. But when you're making split-second decisions that your life depends on, it's easy to forget such things.

Well, I joked, trying to break the tension, *we can always ride the camel.* And right then, he shook himself and bolted off in the opposite direction, as if he'd understood me.

Ruby glanced at the gauge and began driving again. *We've got a couple of kilometres left in us yet.* We headed along the track, which was still following the curves of the river. *Keep your eye out for a place to camp,* she said, *that can't be seen from the trail.*

I pointed to a smaller track that led directly down to the bank, but, when Ruby climbed out and inspected the area, it was obvious even to me that there wasn't enough foliage to hide our van. We kept heading in the same direction, the windscreen wipers slapping back and forth. Soon, a big modern house, perched on top of a huge, cleared rise, came into view. Two Range Rovers were parked under a carport beside it. At the back was a large barn made of aluminium siding. There were three ponies in the yard and a bunch of ducks waddling around a pond. I didn't like the look of the place and I could tell by the way Ruby frowned that she didn't like it, either. The dairy farmer who lived there must have been the same one who'd nailed up a *No Camping* sign about a kilometre back. It didn't seem fair that he and his family and a bunch of cows could have so much land all to themselves and yet not share it with a single person who needed to light a fire or sleep under a tree for a night.

I was glad to see the homestead disappear in the rear-view mirror, but knowing there was a dairy farmer close by made our task even harder. Ruby slowed the van to a crawl. I didn't know whether it was because we were down to our last few trickles of petrol, or if she was becoming more desperate to find a camping spot immediately. The baby began wriggling in my arms, wanting to get down on the floor. She'd wet her nappy again and was stinking something awful. I was just starting to think we'd have to take our chances with the farmer – that we'd have to pull over and camp anywhere, even beside the trail. But right at that moment, to my left, I glimpsed a flash of blue amongst the trees and vines. I told Ruby to stop and back up a little, which she did. I pointed to what I'd seen and she leaned over and peered out my window. It was overgrown with weeds and vines and the front door had fallen off, but about twenty metres back from the track stood an old, derelict wooden cottage surrounded by bushes and trees.

Ruby drove slowly through the long grass towards it. Dead branches cracked under the wheels and at one point I had to jump from the van and move a log out of our way. The sun was sinking and the twilight chill stung my face. I cleared a rough path so that Ruby could drive around and park at the back of the cottage.

Inside, it was cold and damp and smelled mouldy. There was an old pot-bellied stove in the kitchen. Some slats of the wooden flooring had fallen away. The two small bedrooms were empty but for pages of yellowing newspaper. Most of the windows were broken. In the main room — which had probably been a living room — there was a stone hearth filled with the charred remains of a fire. Two half-burnt cigarette packets sat beside it, along with several rusting beer cans and an empty cardboard cask of Coolabah. Someone — or several people — had been here before us, but it didn't look like they were going to return any time soon.

Ruby changed the baby, while I walked outside to gather wood. Most of it was wet, however. The gum leaves were beaded with rainwater and the few fallen logs were covered in moss. I scouted the immediate area, but the only dry kindling I could find was under the veranda of the house — a few twigs and branches, but certainly not enough to get a fire going. I looked around, thinking maybe I'd have to pull some planks up from the porch, when I suddenly remembered that Roy's prosthetic was still in the van. I grabbed it from the back and marched into the house. I balled up the old newspaper and built a pyramid of sticks, and within ten minutes a fire was crackling in the hearth. Ruby smiled as I picked up the leg and chucked it into the flames. The flesh-coloured paint curled and melted. We sat silently, watching it blacken and smoulder. The toes went first. Within minutes they were merely a row of pulsing embers. It was curiously calming to watch the carved initials and names of Roy's mates and the memory of that small town slowly being reduced to a mound of grey ash.

I unpacked our bedding and spread it out in front of the fire, now stoked with some floorboards I'd pulled up from the kitchen. For a while we just sat there, resting and warming ourselves and trying to figure out what to do. I could tell Ruby was buggered, so, before it became completely dark, I grabbed our plastic container, and crept through the forest to the river. After scooping up some fresh water, I heated some up on the fire, along with three of our last six cans of food.

By the time we finished eating, the night was all around us. I looked through the window frames and saw nothing but a pale half-moon, just visible through the clouds. Rain pattered against the tin roof. When the wind blew, branches scratched against the side of the house. I hugged my knees and stared into the fire, trying to think of a way we could get out of the National Park and away from Roy forever. It wouldn't be long before the farmer discovered us and started asking questions.

Ruby found a half-smoked cigarette near the hearth and lit it up. She lay beside the sleeping baby, leaning on one elbow, inhaling deeply. I could tell she was deep in thought. I wondered whether she was concerned with our immediate problem or if she was thinking about our bastard of a father and how he could do such a thing to Mum. Ruby knew Roy better than anyone. She'd always been his favourite, and not just because she could drive a truck or shoot a bird out of the sky. Maybe it was a first-born thing, or because she was a girl. Not that they didn't have fights – oh, they had some doozies, over boys, over curfews, over the remote control –

but Ruby was able to reason with Roy in a way that Mum and I never could, and it was just a mysterious thing to me the way she could sometimes calm him down.

She took one last drag and threw the butt in the fire, and that's when I decided I'd take my chance and ask her. We hadn't discussed what had happened back home in any detail and I was feeling heavy and confused.

Ruby, why do you think he did it? I asked. *How could he do that to her?*

Her face was flushed from the fire, which made her look younger and gentler than she usually seemed. *How the fuck would I know, Mark? The guy's a maniac.*

And I knew then that I couldn't get any more out of her. She probably thought it had been a stupid question, that any sensible person shouldn't be surprised that such a violent marriage ended in the way that it did.

Of course, I assumed Ruby was tougher than I, that she took each bad thing that happened to us in her stride. But later that night, when we lay dozing by the embers, I heard her weeping softly.

We woke early to the chirping of birds. They trilled and piped in the trees outside, as if they'd all just received some wonderful news. I walked out the back and could see three red-tailed cockatoos perched in the branches of a peppermint gum, and several honeyeaters swaying on banksia blossoms. It was still lightly drizzling and the rainforest smelled damp and fresh. I went back inside and pulled up some more old floorboards from the kitchen and lit another fire. There was a chance the dairy farmer would notice the smoke curling out of the chimney, but it was so cold that Ruby and I were willing to take the risk.

As she heated up some hot water for coffee, I could see my sister's face had returned to its usual hard expression. It was difficult to imagine that she was the same girl who'd been crying in the dark a few hours before. Of course, I didn't mention it – she would have thumped me if I had – but it did make me wonder what was going on in that head of hers, why she never let down her guard and why she had to act as if she was always in control.

After her cup of instant coffee, she stood up and told me to wait in the cottage and mind the baby, who was fingering a crack in the floor. When I asked her where she was going, she didn't answer, just walked straight out the front door and down the steps, swinging her skinny arms as if she owned the entire property. I stood at the window and watched her grow smaller as she blended into the wet forest. The vines and bushes eventually swallowed her up and, for one terrible moment, I was convinced I would never see her again, that she'd be bitten by a snake or, even worse, that she'd decided to abandon me and the baby altogether and find a way to Sydney and our aunt without having to worry about us.

I busied myself by changing my little sister and feeding her half a tin of warm chicken soup. She began crawling around the cottage, picking up bits of dirt and dead beetles and trying to put them in her mouth. She'd never crawled that much at home, preferring to stay in her baby bouncer and stare at the television.

Ruby was gone a long time, more than an hour. I kept looking through the front-door frame, hoping to glimpse her wild red hair, her tough long face, in the distance. But all I saw were cows moving along the trail, pulling at weeds and grass. I distracted myself by trying to teach the baby her first word. At home, we'd tried to coax her to say 'Mum' or 'Ma' every day for the past few months, but at fifteen months she still hadn't uttered anything more complicated than a gurgling baby babble. And now, of course, there didn't seem to be any point in teaching her that name, so instead I attempted to teach her to say 'Mark', which wasn't too different from 'Ma'.

Ruby finally returned with her wet windcheater balled up in her arms. She gently lowered it onto the floor and spread it flat. As she did so, six brown eggs were revealed. *Stole 'em from the chicken coop*, she announced, grinning. A few white feathers were stuck to her wet hair and her face was streaked with mud.

What about the farmer? I asked. *Did you run into him?*

Ruby grabbed the baby and lifted her onto her lap. *Waited till he pissed off in his four-wheel-drive.* Then she lowered her voice, as if she didn't even want the birds to hear. *Listen, Mark. I've been checking out the farm. Now I'll tell you how we're going to get out of here.*

I guess the first time you have to do something new is always the hardest. Like when Roy made me skin a possum or eat sheep's balls. Both times I vomited — I was only nine — yet, in the following year, I went on to skin several rabbits and eat even weirder things, like boiled bull's eyes and entrails.

I had to remind myself of this when, late that night, Ruby led me across the paddock behind the farmer's house. It had finally stopped raining and I could see the Southern Cross twinkling in the sky. We'd put the baby to sleep and locked her inside one of the bedrooms so she wouldn't get into any trouble. She rarely woke at night, anyway. I had a flashlight in my hand but I didn't dare turn it on. Ruby had the knife and two plastic containers.

The barn door wasn't locked. We let ourselves in and closed it behind us. Inside, the air was stale and heavy, and smelled of engine oil and manure. I flicked on the torch and the pale beam lit up a bulldozer, a tractor and a mini motorbike. Metal shelves lined the walls and were filled with all sorts of tools: power drills, spanners, boxes of nails and screws. One lower shelf held just gardening equipment: forks and spades, fertiliser, seeds sealed in paper envelopes. On the floor was a green hose with a sprinkler still attached to the end. When Ruby saw it, she flashed me a smile.

She unscrewed the sprinkler and cut a length of about two metres from the hose. In the half-light, it looked as if she were severing a snake or the tentacle of an octopus. We walked around all the vehicles and decided the tractor would be our best bet. Ruby figured it ran on the same fuel as our van.

Luckily, the fuel caps of farm equipment don't come with any locks. I don't know when Ruby realised this – maybe when she was sneaking around the farm earlier in the day. I can't say I felt confident as she unscrewed the cap and fed the hose through the hole and into the tank. She passed me the end of it and took the torch from my hand.

OK, Mark, she said, *you're on*, like I was some nervous singer who didn't want to appear on stage.

I would have preferred having to perform in front of a thousand people than being forced to do what I had to do next. I put the hose in my mouth, but, catching just a whiff of the fumes, I gagged.

Hurry up, urged Ruby. *Suck.*

I exhaled and pressed my lips around the rubber tubing.

Just pretend it's a straw, she added. *A jumbo straw. You're drinking a thickshake. A double chocolate thickshake.*

My eyes were watering. I counted to three and began to draw in my breath.

Instead of following Ruby's advice, I pretended I was inhaling from a pipe, not the kind Sherlock Holmes smoked, but one of those hookah pipes that Arabians used in harems. I'd seen them in old movies on TV: huge urns with a looping hose attached and a gold mouthpiece. The men would sit cross-legged on cushions and pass it around while veiled women hovered in the background or even danced with flowing scarves.

I was just imagining what it would be like to be one of those men when my mouth suddenly burned with a hot rush of metallic-tasting liquid. I gagged and spat it out but already it felt as if my lungs were on fire. Ruby snatched the hose away and pushed the end of it into the plastic container sitting on the ground. I could feel the chemical vapour flaring through my nostrils, my ears, my throat. I coughed and retched and finally threw up the two boiled eggs I'd had for dinner. By the time I'd found the tap outside and had rinsed my mouth, we had nearly eight litres of petrol.

We were back on the logging track within half an hour. Even Ruby wanted to escape that dairy farm as soon as possible and find a telephone box. We headed north, towards the Bruxner Highway. It was past midnight by then and we both knew there'd be few cars on the road and even less cops around. Still, I was nervous about the idea of being on a highway, about accidentally running into Roy again. The baby lay asleep in my arms, wrapped in a blanket. The track was wet and slippery from the rain and I could tell by the way Ruby pursed her lips as she steered that she was absolutely determined not to make a mistake and cause us another accident. In her own way, she was silently saying to me, *See, Mark? This is the way you do it.* But since I'd siphoned the petrol all on my own, I didn't feel so bad about having crashed the van.

We hit the highway about an hour later, and I was relieved that Ruby turned right so that we were now heading towards Casino, which also meant we were driving towards Lismore, Ballina and the coast. There were mostly semis on the highway but they sped right past us, like big, roaring monsters.

The first town to appear was Tabulam, which was so small it had only one pub, a church and a general store.

Outside the store, a telephone box stood glowing in the night like a golden mirage. Ruby parked and opened the door. *I'll handle this*, she said, fishing in her pocket for some change. She circled the van and entered the box. I watched her pick up the receiver and, by the way her shoulders slumped, I could tell the phone was out of order.

As she climbed back into the van, she muttered, *Fucking vandals*, even though, between us, we'd probably destroyed the public telephone back home five or six times and had enjoyed every moment of it.

There was nothing else to do but head over the Clarence River and continue on to Casino. I'd never been there before and wondered aloud if it was anything like the movies and pictures I'd seen of Las Vegas.

Don't be stupid, said Ruby. *It was probably named after some rich dago who bought up the land and cut down the trees. Giuseppe Casino or somebody like that.*

This didn't seem very plausible either, but I kept my mouth shut. It did no good to argue with Ruby when she was in one of her moods. I couldn't blame her, of course. She was tired of driving, and sarcasm was her way of dealing with stress.

The clouds were clearing and I could see faint stars in the sky. I was thinking that we were only half an hour away from an entirely new plan for the rest of our lives. I didn't think Aunty Candy would want us to continue driving to Sydney on our own. She could be pretty wild but she wasn't that crazy, especially when it came to her sister's kids. No, she'd probably tell us to sit tight and would wire us some money in the morning. Ruby could sign for it and we'd travel in luxury by bus or train to Sydney.

These ideas were still forming in my mind when we reached the outskirts of Casino. I imagined us sitting in a dining car and ordering baked dinners, sleeping in our own compartment on fold-out beds, the sea and shimmering beaches rushing by.

The town was flat and deserted and, when Ruby pulled up beside a closed café, the only thing we could hear was a dog barking in the distance. The main street was a line of dark shopfronts wreathed in iron lace. A rusty sign swung from an awning, squeaking back and forth in the wind. I couldn't imagine any place more different from Las Vegas – Casino was more like a ghost town where even the ghosts had fled to a better place.

Ruby spotted a phone box on the next corner and strode straight down to it without saying a word to me. The glass walls of the box were cracked but I could still see her clearly. I watched her pick up the receiver and insert some coins. She waited a few moments, bowed her head slightly and began speaking into the mouthpiece. There was a pause. I imagined that hollow, windy sound just before the operator connects you to the number you've requested, and then the rhythm of Candy's ring tone in my ear, and then her voice, *Hello, darling!* She always said that, no matter who was calling.

But from what I could see, this wasn't happening at all. Ruby was frowning and twisting the telephone cord around her finger. Her shoulders were hunched and she looked as if she was in the midst of an argument. Finally, she smashed the receiver against one of the glass walls of the phone box and kicked open the door.

When she climbed back into the van, I was almost too scared to ask her what had happened.

Phone's disconnected, she said, turning on the ignition. *Stupid bitch mustn't have paid her bill.*

4

It had nothing to do with gangrene or axes. Roy Stamp used to get pissed at the pub and make up stories about himself. He was a bad seed from a good family and couldn't stand being as ordinary as the rest of us. He was the first person in this town to buy a sack of manure with a Visa card. He'd chase his beer with a nip of vodka. For a while there, back in the '80s, he wore a white panama hat with a black band. So you can see he had tickets on himself.

Just after New Year, he vanished from the pub for about three months. Of course, everyone was worried and rumours flew. During his disappearance, Sapphire wouldn't let anyone set foot inside their house, just talked through the locked screen door. When we went to visit to find out what was wrong, she was always barefoot and wearing a housecoat. She looked tired and her hair was unbrushed. She'd say that Roy had been travelling a lot and had been off the booze, then she'd close the door before we could ask any more questions.

Of course, that set tongues wagging. No one had seen or heard of Roy in a long, long time. The boy, Mark, had been sent away to *foster care, and the girl hardly ever went to school. We all wondered what was going on in that run-down old house. After Sapphire had closed the door on us, we'd walk around the back and pretend we were admiring the orchard, but really we would be sniffing around for some evidence of foul play.*

We never smelled dead bodies or anything like that. All the curtains in the house were drawn. Roy's semi was nowhere to be seen. We all knew he had a keen eye for the ladies and figured that he'd probably shot through with another girl and Sapphire was just too damn proud to admit that she'd been dumped.

As it turned out, all that time, Roy had been in Brisbane Hospital, recovering from his injuries. He'll tell you that his truck broke down on the highway. He'll brag about how he jumped a freight train heading back this way. He'll say he amused himself by jumping from one carriage to another, like a cowboy in a movie, and, when the train took a sudden turn, he lost his balance and slipped between the carriages, when what really happened was he got drunk one night in the Macksville pub and fell asleep on the train tracks while he was trying to find where he parked his rig. That's how he lost his leg. That's how ordinary Roy Stamp really is.

When your options suddenly vanish, there are only two things you can do: give up and surrender to the people who took your freedom away, or rebel against the whole lot and go for broke. I'd already explained to Ruby that there was no way I was going back into foster care, that I'd rather die on the road than end up back in some remote hick town with a family of inbred, lard-arsed losers. Ruby didn't take much convincing. She hated the idea of the government telling her where to go and what to do, even more than I did. And besides, she reasoned, we were only minors, so, no matter how many laws we ended up breaking, if we were ever caught, we could just plead not guilty and blame everything on our father because of the years of abuse we'd suffered.

Gradually, a lot of the stress and fear we'd been feeling began to disappear. Sure, Candy's disconnected phone was a setback, but that didn't mean she wasn't alive and well and still living in Kings Cross. Apparently, it wasn't a big place – she'd often described it as a little village – so we had nothing to lose by heading south at our own pace and trying to track her down. We now had a method of obtaining free petrol; Ruby and I were both good at shoplifting; and we could drive at night, when we couldn't be recognised.

We studied the map and decided to follow the highway east and keep driving until daylight. Ruby and I had napped earlier in the day, back at the cottage, and now that our lives had opened up to us in such an unexpected way and we were free to do as we wished, without adults interfering, we both felt excited and alive. Even the baby sat upright in my arms, watching the streetlights flash by, as if she were counting every one of them.

I peeled the last boiled egg we had, fed it to her, and gave her a drink of water. I remember thinking about the first time I ever saw my baby sister, when she was about six weeks old. Roy had picked me up in his Fairlane from my foster family in Wee Waa, and driven me home, mostly in silence. After not seeing me for twelve months, the only thing he said to me was, *I hope you've learned your lesson.* I nodded, not looking at him, not even knowing what lesson I was supposed to have learned. That day was also the first time I'd seen his wooden leg. When I asked him what had happened, he just grunted and told me he'd had an accident on the road. When we stopped for petrol, it was strange to see him hobbling about the service station like an old man. I actually felt sorry for him.

We pulled up in front of the house just before dinner time. Mum was sitting out on the veranda, wearing a midnight-blue dress. Her black hair was pulled up and styled into a roll, with a sprig of jasmine pinned to the side. It was dusk, and she was bathed in a pale, silvery light. I couldn't remember a time in my life when I'd seen her look more beautiful or serene. And she had some sort of bundle in her arms, but of course I didn't know then what it was – Roy hadn't mentioned a thing during the five-hour drive.

I bounded up the steps and hugged her tight. I'd missed my mother more than anyone or anything in the world, more than my friends at school, my football team, or my set of favourite films taped from the television. She'd written to me, of course, and I'd written back, but even she had failed to mention that she'd had another baby.

When I first saw my new sister, I kind of fell in love. She had Mum's green eyes and long dark eyelashes, and a little frown above the bridge of her nose. Her hair was a mass of thick red curls. When she looked up at me, she smiled, like she recognised who I was and had been waiting to meet me her whole short life.

We wanted to surprise you! said Mum, hugging me with her free arm and kissing me over and over. And, while Roy limped straight up the front steps and into the house, Mum passed the baby over to me and I held her and inhaled her powdery scent for the first time. It was so good to be home, even if it meant living with my father.

As Ruby and I sped down the highway, I thought about how strange it was that such a gorgeous little creature like the baby could have sprung from the loins of Roy Stamp. It was like Frankenstein's monster fathering Tinkerbell, or Count Dracula planting the seed that created Little Red Riding Hood. But then again, Ruby and I had come from the very same place, and neither of us had inherited our father's mean, violent nature. Oh sure, Ruby could be rude and sarcastic, but when the shit hit the fan she could also be kind and fiercely protective, and as we headed towards the coast that day, I couldn't help but admire her dogged effort to get us away from our father and into a better life.

By the time we hit the Pacific Highway, we'd travelled about one hundred k's, and it was raining once again. Ruby didn't want to stop and camp in the wet, so, instead of heading east another five kilometres to the beach, we remained on the highway, heading towards Grafton. Every now and then, the windscreen would fog up and I'd have to wipe it clear with a rag. Now that we were on a major road, I noticed Ruby was much more attentive to her driving. She constantly checked the various speed limits, careful not to drive too fast or too slow, and kept looking in the rear-view mirror to make sure another car or driver didn't get too close to us and our van. The visor of Roy's cap, as usual, was pulled down over her forehead – her hair was tucked up beneath the elastic, and I imagined that from a distance she looked like a skinny farmer taking his son and daughter on a camping trip.

By dawn, we'd reached the fishing village of Maclean, which lay between a lake and a wide river, only about half an hour from the coastal town of Yamba. It was still raining, but we both knew it was too dangerous to drive any further now that full daylight was approaching. Instead of heading through town, we followed a track that ran beside the river until we found a secluded spot to park.

We crawled into the back and slept for several hours. I had weird dreams about trying to run really fast but my legs wouldn't work properly and I felt as if I were wading through quicksand. I woke up before Ruby and the baby, who were curled up together beneath a blanket. The rain had stopped. I climbed out of the van and decided to look around.

The area was much greener than our hometown. Willow trees bowed over the river. The grass smelled fresh and sweet. I walked along the bank for a while, picking dandelions. I was starving by then and ate two or three and saved the rest for Ruby. At a slight bend, I walked to the edge of the bank, kneeled and scooped up some water to drink, and that is when I discovered them: three large ceramic pots bobbing in the current, tied to a fallen log.

I lifted one up and peered into it, and what I saw seemed miraculous, as if some guardian angel or even God had placed the pots there for me to find at that very moment. Inside were three or four crabs scuttling back and forth, pincers still clipping at the air. The second pot had just as many; and the third, only two. I tipped them all into the first pot, untied it from the log, and half-ran back to the van, before the fisherman who'd placed them there realised he'd been robbed.

By the time my sisters woke up, at around midday, I'd already started a fire. I noticed the baby was sleeping even more than usual and wondered if she was ill. When Ruby saw all the crabs, she slapped me hard on the back and, even though it hurt, I was glad of her approval. We boiled them up in an old kerosene can and sat cross-legged on the ground, cracking the shells and picking out the soft white flesh with our fingers.

Even though it was still cloudy, I could already feel how much warmer it was here than at home. The sun came out briefly and shone on the back of my neck. For the first time I wondered if it was possible that our mother could still be with us, that there might be some kind of afterlife that allowed her to shadow her children. Maybe she was in the sunlight on my skin, or in the breeze that blew through the stalks of paspalum. Maybe she could distil herself into the raindrops that fell on my head and made my hair all stiff and curly. Perhaps she'd somehow led Ruby to the farmer's tractor and me to the crab pots, and it was only her body that was left behind in Roy's shed, like a piece of rotting meat.

If this were so, I wondered if I could communicate with her more directly, like those mediums on TV who talk to the dead. They pick someone out of the audience and tell them all sorts of things: *Your husband still loves you. I'm seeing a grey-haired woman with glasses. I'm sensing someone here today who has lost a child.* And people nod and start weeping and ask the medium to relay special messages to the ghosts on the other side.

Ruby, I asked, *have you ever had a séance?*

Ruby nodded. *Over at Patty Roden's one night. She had a Ouija board.*

Did you contact any spirits?

She nodded again. *Patty's grandfather, Horace.*

What did he say?

He said Patty was beautiful and that she'd grow up and marry a really rich man.

I crossed my legs and looked at the sky. *Wow*, I said, marvelling at how easy it was to talk with the dead. *Did you contact anyone else?*

Yep, replied Ruby, tossing a crab shell into the fire. *We had a long conversation with Adolf Hitler.*

Hitler? I could hardly believe what I was hearing. *What did he say?*

He agreed with Horace. Patty was really beautiful and she was going to grow up and marry a rich man.

I chewed on the insides of my cheeks. Surely Hitler would have more important things to comment on than silly Patty Roden.

She's not even pretty, I said, before I could stop myself.

And that's when Ruby snorted and fell on her side, laughing. *Oh, come on, Mark. There were four of us with our fingers on the plastic thing that spells out the letters. Patty was moving it around the whole time.*

I picked up a rock and smashed the shell of another crab. I hated it when Ruby made fun of me, especially when I was trying to be serious. *Well, just because Patty's an idiot, doesn't mean they don't work.*

What?

I sighed and stretched my legs. *Séances.*

Ruby shook her head. *That stuff's a lot of crap. You know, I don't even believe in astrology. I mean, I'm a Scorpio and that bitch Debbie Dinning is a Scorpio – we're born only two days apart – and look how different we are!*

I thought of Debbie Dinning with her sharp tongue, short skirts, and string of boyfriends. In fact, she and Ruby seemed very much alike – except that Debbie came from a rich family – but I kept this opinion to myself. And I realised then that if there was any way to communicate with the spirit of my mother, I would have to discover it by myself, without the help or interference of my sister.

We spent the rest of the day wandering around the town, taking turns carrying the baby. It was an old-fashioned place with wide verandas that stretched out over the footpaths. Some of the shop windows were gilded with ornate gold lettering and others had little bells that rang when the doors were pushed open. In one store I stole a reel of fishing line and some hooks. In another, chocolate bars and mixed dried fruit. It was easy shoplifting with the baby in tow. If the attendant was a woman, Ruby would distract her by going up to the counter and making the baby smile and clap her hands, and then there'd be lots of *goo-goo* and *ga-ga* talk and the attendant would ask how old she was and tell Ruby about her own children, while I fleeced the shelves for things I thought we would need. If we found a man behind the counter, I'd take the baby with me and slip items beneath her wrap, while Ruby flirted with the guy, no matter how old he was – even fifty.

My heart sank, however, when we stepped out of a pharmacy and it was raining again. It wasn't just raining, it was bucketing down, so much so that we could barely see the footpath on the other side of the street. Further down the block, a small crowd had gathered outside an old pub. At first, I thought maybe they were playing two-up, or perhaps someone had had an accident. We strolled down to where they were gathered, and discovered a teenage boy who was walking on his hands. His face was very red and his knees were bent above him, so he looked like this human question mark hobbling along the footpath. Kids were laughing and I heard a woman say, *What a freak!* He had an upturned baseball cap on the footpath. Suddenly the kid did a back flip and was on his feet again. He picked up the cap and held it out to the crowd, who clapped and dropped in coins. His face was swollen scarlet, but he was grinning widely, like he'd just won an Oscar and was preparing to make a speech. He was pretty tall and skinny, about Ruby's age, or maybe a bit older, with black curly hair and eyes the colour of dark honey. Ruby riffled around her pocket and dropped a coin into his cap. He smiled at her directly and murmured something – I didn't understand it – and Ruby smiled back, as if she recognised what he'd said.

What'd you do that for? I asked, angry at her for wasting what little money we had.

Ruby started walking up the stairs of the pub. *He's cute.*

She left me with the baby while she went to use the Ladies'. Fortunately, there were a few other kids in the pub with their mothers, drinking lemonade and throwing around a piece of green sponge shaped like a football. I sat in a corner, near the snack bar. I waited five, ten minutes but Ruby didn't return. Someone had left half a middy of beer on the table, so I picked it up and drank it. It made me feel dizzy and relaxed. I looked out the window and all I could see was that kid's feet bobbing back and forth – an upside-down pair of worn cowboy boots dancing above the sill. A woman came around, emptying ashtrays, and smiled at me and the baby. I glanced at the clock above the bar; Ruby had been gone over a quarter of an hour. I was just about to find the Ladies' and see what was wrong with her when she finally appeared, looking fresh and scrubbed, her hair wet and still dripping down her back.

Where've you been? I hissed.

But Ruby just smiled and sat opposite me. *If you go upstairs, you'll find empty single rooms, with clean towels, and an old bathroom with hot water.*

I couldn't believe her daring. It was one thing to steal a

packet of chips, but quite another to walk straight into a hotel in a strange town and start using its facilities.

Shit, Ruby, you could have got caught. We're not even supposed to be in here without our parents.

Ruby shrugged. *We'll tell them they're dead. At least it'd be half true. Go on*, she added, *I dare you.*

I had this feeling she was up to something, but I wasn't sure what, like she was trying to get rid of me, or wanted to do something behind my back. I glanced out the window — at least that boy was now gone, and the rain was beginning to ease.

I don't feel like a shower, I said. *I'm hungry.*

We returned to the van and ate some chocolate. Ruby brushed her wet hair. After that, we all dozed until it was dark. By the time we hit the road, it was raining again and Ruby was in a filthy mood. I was expecting her to pull off the highway and head for the coast, but she steered us down the Pacific Highway, as if she had no choice, as if the van was driving her rather than the other way around.

She must have known what I was thinking. *No point going to the beach in this weather. We'll go through Grafton and head for Coffs.*

I turned on our torch and studied the map. Coffs Harbour was about a hundred and fifty kilometres away, and I figured if all went well, we'd be at the coast in a couple of hours.

The windscreen wipers had a hypnotic effect on the baby and she began dozing in my arms. I found myself nodding off, too, dreaming of foaming surf.

I only woke when Ruby pulled over on the highway. *What's up?* I said, as cars zoomed past us. She didn't answer, but stuck her head out the window and waved. I looked in the rear-view mirror and saw a guy running towards us.

What the hell are you doing, Ruby? I could see he was carrying a cricket kit bag. By this time, the baby was awake as well. *Are you nuts?* I persisted. *We can't pick anyone up.*

The guy ran along Ruby's side of the van and stopped just short of the door. I was scared by now, even though I couldn't see him. He could be a serial killer for all we knew. But Ruby just leaned out the window, and asked, ever-so-sweetly, *Do you know how to drive?*

I heard his voice above the roar of traffic. *Haven't got my licence but I could handle this thing.*

Ruby turned and reached over the seat. She clicked the lever and the side door slid open. *Get in*, she said. And that was when I recognised him, that grinning smartarse from back in Maclean who walked on his hands for money.

5

We're what you call dick sisters. Most of us have been related since way back in high school, but we've had a few more additions to the sisterhood over the years. Of course, back in those days, girls didn't talk about that sort of thing with each other, so we didn't know we were sisters until we were all grown up and married to other men.

The last two years of high school Roy was dating Sapphire Tate, but it was easy for some of us to see he liked a bit on the side. Years later, it took all of us getting drunk at a lingerie party for it to come out. Jo-Jo started it by blurting out that, when she was sixteen, Roy Stamp went down on her in the back of the gym after a sports carnival. Tiffany blushed and said that she'd sucked his cock twice after his team had won the regional footy championship. There was a long silence then and someone murmured, Poor Sapphire. But it wasn't long before Ebony confessed that Roy Stamp had been her brother's best friend and that he used to creep into her room at night, tie her wrists to the bed head, and fuck her from behind. Felicity thought he was a dud root. Pam announced he had a big member, but Roxanne insisted his tackle was small and he couldn't last the distance.

The only ones who hadn't confessed to the sisterhood were Olga, who'd been born with polio; Tina, who had a thyroid problem and had always been twice her healthy weight; and then there was Clare, who'd been our student teacher for about six months before she suddenly resigned and got engaged. She was sitting there clutching her daiquiri and looking so red-faced we thought she would burst. She was still pretty, in a Laura Ashley kind of way — you know, not much make-up, lace collars, her shoes always matched her handbag. We all thought she'd been a virgin till she married Tom Hopkins at the age of twenty-one and went to Cairns on her honeymoon.

But we could all tell by the way Clare was blinking back tears and struggling to remain calm that she'd been rattled by our stories. We knew then that something more serious had occurred between her and Roy, more serious than a quickie down by the swimming hole or a blow-job in the orchards. We asked her what had happened, but she seemed offended by our questions, as if she was above us and Roy Stamp and everything he stood for.

We asked her how many times they'd done it. We questioned her about his hairy arse, the birthmark on his shoulder, how he growls like a dog when he comes. And the more we teased her, the more upset she became, like she was scared we were second-guessing her deepest secrets and would tell the whole world and her husband and kids. We accused her of having fallen in love with Roy Stamp while he'd been her student, but we'll never know for sure because she picked up her bag and stormed out of the party. She got into her car and drove out of our lives, and *since then, the only times we see her are when she's in the checkout at Woolworths.*

But this is the funny thing: only three days after the lingerie party, at the start of the new year, Roy Stamp disappeared for a couple of months, and, at the same time, Clare's Toyota ended up in the garage at Tenterfield Automotive. The mechanic told us the bonnet and one side were dented and that there was blood all over the front and the right tyre. Clare had explained to him that she'd hit a roo on the highway. But when Roy turned up at the pub about ten weeks later with his right leg missing, and when we thought back and did the sums about when Clare's car accident occurred, it was obvious to all of us that she was a dick sister, too; that she'd run him down, trying to kill him, still jealous after all these years.

I knew he'd be trouble from the moment he crawled into the van. He told us he was fifteen years old but he acted like he'd been around the world three times and even a few other places in between. He poked his head between our seats and talked non-stop. He lived with his aunt in Tweed Heads but was hitchhiking to Melbourne. His mother had run off with a man and he hadn't seen her in two years. Before that, his mother had stolen a car in Sydney and they'd travelled around the country together like Bonnie and Clyde. He knew how to shoplift. He reckoned he could read minds. All this he told us before he even mentioned his own name or thought to ask us where we were headed.

Ruby was tired of driving and the kid offered to take over. But instead of stopping and changing places, she made me and the baby get into the back and told the smartarse to sit in the passenger seat. Then they did this complicated manoeuvre: while she continued to drive, she raised her bum off the seat and the kid slid beneath her and took over the pedals. For a few moments they were both driving and his hands were on hers as they steered the van and laughed. It was a stupid and dangerous thing to do and I told Ruby so, but she just slid off his lap and told me to shut up.

I'll have to give him this: the kid was a good driver. He changed lanes with ease, even overtook a couple of cars, and didn't talk as much when he had to do things like that. Ruby was interested in how much money he'd made walking on his hands back in Maclean.

Five dollars a minute, he said, which to me seemed highly unlikely. *No matter where I do it, it always averages out to five dollars a minute.*

So how long did you do it for? said Ruby.

The kid shrugged. *I made fifty-four dollars and seventy cents. So, I guess between ten and eleven minutes.*

Just for walking on your hands? I asked.

No, the kid replied. *They also pay to see my fabulous good looks.*

Ruby thought that was hilarious and laughed and slapped her leg. She really had terrible taste in boys, and this one was just another addition to the long line of weirdos she always fell for. She once went with a guy who played the banjo with his feet. And another one who'd tattooed a moustache onto his face.

I asked the kid why he was hitching to Melbourne.

I'm going to meet the King and Queen of Sweden.

Yeah, I said, *and I'm going to Siberia.*

I've got an invitation, he added. *From the Swedish Consulate.*

I rolled my eyes, but I could tell Ruby not only believed what he saying but was even more impressed by him.

What are you going to do when you meet them? I asked. *Walk on your hands?*

I'll practise my Swedish. Det är dåligt väder.

That's not Swedish. You made that up.

Not everyone's as dumb as you are, Mark, snapped Ruby. Then she turned to him and said, *Say something else.*

Du har vacker öga.

What does that mean?

You have beautiful eyes.

Ruby giggled like a child and edged closer to him. She finally introduced herself and me, and the kid told us his name was Duke.

Duke? I said. *What kind of name is that?*

But I never got to hear the answer because at that moment we all saw trouble ahead. Cars were banked up for about half a kilometre and we could see the blue lights of several police cars flashing in the distance. We were just outside of Grafton.

Uh oh, said Ruby. Duke slowed down and murmured something to himself. Some drivers were turning around and heading back the way they came. Others were honking their horns. I noticed one truck ahead of us turning right off the highway and heading up a narrow road and, before even consulting us or asking our permission, Duke swung a hard right and followed it.

Listen, Duke, I said. *We're headed for Coffs Harbour.*

Well, what do you expect him to do? asked Ruby. *Drive straight into the roadblock?*

The beams of the headlights shook as the van jolted over potholes. *Honey and I drove this road once,* said Duke. *Some of the most beautiful countryside I've ever seen.*

I noticed Ruby stiffen. *Who's Honey?* she asked sharply.

Oh, he said. *A girl I once knew. We stole a car and fooled around in the forest.*

The truck ahead of us turned off on to a dirt track, but Duke kept heading along the bitumen road. I began to feel scared and suspicious, thinking that maybe the roadblock we'd just avoided had been set up to catch a dangerous criminal, and that the person the cops were after just might be now driving our van into the wilderness to hurt or maybe kill us all.

Ruby began playing with her hair. *What's there to see?*

Crystal-clear rivers. Huge willow trees. Mountains, said Duke. The bitumen road ended and we bumped on to a narrow gravel track.

We're supposed to be heading south, I said, growing more impatient.

Well, we can't go bloody south, said Ruby. *Those cops'll probably be there all night.* She turned back to Duke. *Can you swim in the rivers?*

Sure! Once Honey and I rode an inner tube down the rapids. It was like a rollercoaster.

It's too cold to swim, I said. *It's the middle of winter.*

Then why're you so gung-ho to get to the beach? asked Ruby.

I sighed but didn't answer. I knew I'd never win, not against those two. There was already a strange bond between them, like they'd been friends for years, or had maybe met in another lifetime. I was angry with Ruby for taking such a risk with this guy, especially after everything we'd been through over the past few days. It wasn't as if we needed any more excitement or complications in our lives. At first, I thought it was just her usual slutty flirtatiousness that had prompted her to pick Duke up, but as he effortlessly changed gears and steered us around sharp bends, and as she slowly revealed the reason we were on the road and what had happened to our mother, I heard a brief choke in her voice and realised she was exhausted by having to always be responsible for me and the baby, by the constant driving, by having to appear as if she was always in control. Duke listened and nodded, making exclamations now and then, and occasionally said things like, *Sounds like my dad.* I could tell she needed someone to take care of her for a while – a shoulder to cry on – and I sensed that person could never be me.

It was slow-going along the track because it was winding and steep. The night was even darker in the forest. After a couple of hours, when we reached Guy Fawkes River, Duke pulled over and we ate more chocolate and chips. He had a sleeping bag stuffed into his cricket bag and, after we finished eating, he climbed out of the van and unrolled it by the stream.

You can sleep in here with us, said Ruby, leaning on the van. Of course, there wasn't enough room, and I was about to object when Duke replied, *I like sleeping under the stars. I even sleep in the backyard at my aunt's*.

Ruby laughed, even though it wasn't funny.

As I lay with the baby in my arms that night, I wondered why Duke had taken the news of our mother's murder so calmly. It was as if he'd been listening to a news report on television, or a story Ruby had half made up. Maybe that was it: he believed and trusted us as little as I did him. I slept restlessly, haunted by these thoughts and the damp smell of the van.

When I woke, the van was empty; not even the baby was by my side. I had visions of Duke abducting my sisters, filling their pockets with rocks and drowning them in the river. I rubbed the sleep out of my eyes and slid open the side door. The sun was slanting through the willows in thin pencils of light and honeyeaters were carolling through the valley. The breeze was crisp and carried the scent of freshly cut grass. It was so tranquil I could feel tension draining out of me.

Ruby was sitting in profile, holding the baby and gazing into a small fire that was burning by the bank of the river. The flames fanned into a smoky orange aura around her silhouette. For a moment, with her slightly bowed head and prominent chin, she looked exactly like our mother, and the image startled me so much I just stood there, staring at the ghostly apparition. I wanted to hold that picture in my mind forever – along with the memory of our mother's pale oval face and the hollows of her collarbone where she always dabbed her perfume — so I could remember it long after my sister, too, was gone from my life forever, when she was lost to a boyfriend or foster care or her own recklessness.

The spell was broken when she turned and said, *I'm starving*. It was only then I could see how straggly her hair was, her smudged cheeks and wrinkled brow.

Where's the Swede? I asked, walking towards the fire.

She shrugged, even though I could see now that she was sitting on his green sleeping bag. *Probably walking up the mountain on his hands.*

We both laughed and I was relieved to sense that her crush on him was already beginning to fade. I picked up a stick and jousted the fire.

He was gone when I got up, she added, stroking the baby's hair. *What a nutcase.*

Yeah, I agreed. *What do you think his game is?*

Ruby chewed on the inside of her cheeks and shrugged again. *At least he can drive. He'll come in handy if we run into any Swedish cops.*

We laughed again. The fire crackled and popped. I was glad to have my sister back, or back as close as we could ever be. *You don't think Roy's set him up to catch us, do you? Paid him to track us down?*

Ruby paused for a moment, gazing into the fire. *Nah*, she said finally. *I don't think he's that smart.*

Who? I asked. *Roy or the Swede?*

Ruby snorted. *Both!* She rearranged the baby in her arms and covered her with the inside of her coat. *But don't worry*, she added, *I'll keep my eye on Duke. If he's any trouble, I'll get rid of him.*

Ruby's resolve not to be hoodwinked by our hitchhiker was a relief, so much so that I relaxed and threw two fishing lines into the river, using bits of Spam for bait.

While I held the lines, I watched the streaming currents, iridescent in the morning light. The nearby ranges were wreathed in mist. I was thinking about our mother again and how much she would have liked this place. She'd been born and raised in mountain country to the northeast of our hometown, near Lamington National Park. Her father had been a horse trainer – one of the best in Queensland – and she'd learned to ride at three years old. By the time she was five, they were taking day trips, then overnight camping adventures, into the Border Ranges and the Lost World Wilderness Area. Aunty Candy – or Brian, as she was known then, and his twin sister, Laura – were teenagers at that point. Brian wasn't interested in camping and by then Laura was in a home for autistics.

Our mother had always told me these weekends were the best parts of her childhood, just her and her father cantering along bush tracks, picnicking by streams, learning to identify various birds and trees. He taught her the difference between a musk lorikeet and a double-eyed fig parrot, and about the many eucalypts. All this had been her paradise until she was eight years old, when her father was thrown by a New Zealand brumby and died of a brain haemorrhage.

Granny was forced to move from the mountains and take a job as a barmaid in our hometown pub, where she and the children boarded upstairs. Our mother continued to love the bush, but she never recovered properly from her father's death, and she never rode a horse again. Some people say that was when her troubles began – her stark depressions and crying jags – and, growing up in a pub with no father around, it was only a matter of time before she attracted more trouble. Brian escaped to Kings Cross, into a netherworld of drugs and sleazebag crooks, while our mother, rumoured to be the prettiest girl in town, fled into a teenage romance with Roy and an unplanned pregnancy. Granny died of breast cancer three days before Mum went into labour.

If Ruby hadn't been conceived, maybe none of all this would have happened – no marriage, no beatings, no corpse in Roy's shed. Maybe even Roy would still have two legs and would be able to drive a semi. But then again, as I sat on the riverbank that morning, I realised that without Ruby's conception, I probably wouldn't have been born, either, or maybe someone else would have been my father. It was too confusing to think about, I decided, and mulling over it couldn't really change anything.

I felt a tugging on one of my lines and began pulling it in. The weight was heavier than I expected and I jumped to my feet for better leverage. I assumed I'd snagged a bit of wood or some other piece of debris, but after a few seconds I was astonished to see silver scales shimmering like sequins on the surface of the water as I reeled in a trout. For a moment, as I lifted it from the river, it performed what looked like a little dance in the air, thrashing its tail back and forth. It writhed and flipped in the grass, gasping, until Ruby grabbed it tightly and cut off its head. She handed the head to me to use for bait later on, and began preparing the fish to cook for breakfast.

After scaling it and steaming it in a pan, she cut the trout in half, reserving a little for the baby, and we sat down together by the fire. We hadn't even taken our first mouthful, however, when Duke emerged from a thicket of trees and came striding towards us. *Went looking for food*, he said. *Could only find these.* He held out a handful of berries. His face was smudged with purplish juice and I wondered how many he'd already eaten.

Ruby sighed with irritation and told him to sit down. She cut a third portion of the trout for Duke and sprinkled the berries over the top. I would have sacrificed the berries for the extra bit of fish but I decided not to say anything.

Trout with fruit tastes pretty strange, but I was so hungry I ate the lot. The baby nearly choked on a bone and Ruby had to thump her on the back to dislodge it from her throat. After that, I gave her a cup of water and settled her on a rug away from the fire, where she sat pulling at the grass and gurgling in her own peculiar language.

We spent the rest of the morning lolling around and playing with the baby. Duke tried to teach her to say his name, but she just smiled and blew bubbles back at him. Then he tried to get her to stand on her own, maybe take her first step, but she kept falling on her bum and rolling sideways. *What's wrong with her?* he asked, easing her back to a sitting position.

Ruby was brushing her hair. *She takes after Mark.*

I picked up a small rock and threw it at Ruby, but missed.

But she doesn't even cry, said Duke.

What's wrong with that?

Well, said Duke, eyeing the baby sideways. *It's not normal.*

Ruby pursed her lips, scowling. She put down the brush, and suddenly rolled on to her back. Her arms and legs began swimming in the air and she started howling and screaming like a tortured infant, as if she'd been starving for days. A flock of frightened honeyeaters took wing. The gum leaves above us seemed to tremble. Her cries echoed through the valley like a siren and I was scared the noise would attract a farmer. Then she stopped wailing just as abruptly, jumped to her feet, and began staggering around the campsite, bumping into the van and the nearby tree, obviously imitating a child taking her first steps, but looking more like a teenager who was hopelessly drunk and who couldn't find her way back home. Her hands clutched at the air as she lurched towards us and, in a high baby voice, she crooned, *Duke! Duke! Duke!* but sounded more like an actress making love in some old B-grade movie. It was one of the funniest things I'd seen in ages and when she fell in a heap the two of us laughed and laughed, while Duke remained as silent and solemn as the baby.

Once we'd quietened down, he asked, not looking at us, *So what's her name again?*

We never told you in the first place, said Ruby.

Top secret, eh?

Oh yeah, said Ruby. *It's so top secret even we don't know what it is.*

Duke frowned, tired of Ruby's games. He fixed his eyes on me.

Mum and Dad couldn't decide on a name, I explained. *So she hasn't been christened yet.*

Duke looked perplexed, but obviously decided to drop the subject. He drew his knees up, hugged them, and murmured something to the baby in Swedish. He then explained how he began to learn the foreign language by watching subtitled films on late-night television. Movies by a guy called Ingmar Bergdorff, or so he said. It was only years later that I realised he'd meant Ingmar Bergman.

So what are his films about? I asked.

Well, they're all different, explained Duke. *There's one where Death plays chess with a knight, one where a father takes revenge on the men who raped his virgin daughter. Another one's about the end of the world.* Then he smiled, looking up at the sky. *The best one's about incest.*

I screwed up my nose. *They sound fucking terrible.*

Duke looked at me as if I was bone ignorant, then shrugged. *The actresses are really cute and they're always topless.*

Ruby snorted. *That'd be right.*

Since he'd begun watching the films, Duke had become interested in all things Swedish, hence his invitation to the consulate to meet the King and Queen.

Why Swedish? I asked. *Why not French or German or ... or Japanese?*

Duke raised his chin. *After I wrote to the Swedish Embassy, the ambassador wrote back to tell me I'm the only person learning Swedish in Australia, that I'm unique!*

He was grinning now and his eyes were glistening. I could tell he felt superior to the millions of people living in this country because he could utter a few foreign phrases.

So, I said, *let's say I took up Swedish, too? How special would you be then?*

Duke bristled. *You're flat out speaking English.*

Du har vacker öga, I said, imitating his guttural accent. *You have beautiful eyes, too.*

Duke set his jaw and glared at me. He muttered something back but didn't bother to translate it.

Ruby asked him why he was hitchhiking, rather than catching a train or a bus to Melbourne.

My aunt wouldn't let me go. She refused to give me the fare.

But you make lots of money walking on your hands.

I have to save for my hotel room, he replied. *And my suit. And also a gift for the King and Queen. Besides, if I hadn't hitched, I wouldn't have met someone like you.*

Ruby smiled and blushed a little, something I'd never seen before. Guys back in our town never said anything like that. They might say, *I wouldn't mind getting into your pants,* or, *That top makes your tits look bigger,* but that was about as far as the flattery would go. Maybe Duke had picked up a few tips from watching all those foreign movies.

Why would the King and Queen want to meet a kid like you? I asked.

He tossed his head and sat up straight. *Because I'm a Duke — it's only natural.*

I snorted and shook my head. *Do they know how young you are?*

He paused for a moment, as if he hadn't considered this question before. *They know how unique I am. That's the main thing.*

I thought he was talking crap but I didn't say anything. At least Ruby was in a better mood.

Duke asked her what star sign she was.

Don't bother, Duke, I said. *She doesn't believe in all that stuff.*

Shut up, Mark, said Ruby. *I never said that.* She turned to Duke. *I'm a Scorpio.* Then she tilted her head to one side, like a dog trying to comprehend a new trick. *So what are they like?*

Duke grinned crookedly, almost lewdly. *They're the sex maniacs of the horoscope.*

Ruby laughed and I noticed her blushing again. She poked the fire with a stick. *What else?*

They have a good sense of humour.

Ruby nodded, pleased by the compliment.

And they have a thing for guys who can walk on their hands.

She laughed again and I shot her a look, a *what the hell are you doing?* expression.

She ignored me and began playing with a lock of her hair. *So what are you?*

Taurus, he said. *Taurus the bull.*

You mean Taurus the bullshit artist, I said.

Just because you don't believe in it, snapped Ruby, *doesn't mean it isn't true.*

I went quiet and leaned back on my elbows. Duke said he knew so much about it because he used to read his mother's stars out to her every day from the *Daily Telegraph.* His mother was into all sorts of weird things: crystals, tarot cards, numerology. She not only talked to trees, she talked to flowers, shrubs, all kinds of animals. She communicated with anything in the universe, he told us, even the ghosts of the dead.

My attention piqued when he said that last bit. *Like what?* I asked. *Like in a séance?*

Duke nodded. *Sometimes.*

Like, with a Ouija board? I asked, looking pointedly at Ruby, who squirmed a little and turned away. She never liked her opinions to be contradicted.

Mum always said those boards were for amateurs. Sometimes she just held a pen loosely in her hand and the ghost would sort of possess her and write down on paper whatever he had to say. Other times she did it more simply.

Like how?

Duke shifted and hugged his knees. *Well, she was always on the lookout for omens.*

What's an omen? asked Ruby.

Well, it's kind of like a sign, said Duke. *Like, whenever she saw two black birds together, whether it was on a fence or a power line, she knew her dead father was nearby or maybe trying to tell her something, because he used to own two black birds in the last years of his life and loved them more than anything.*

This idea seemed pretty kooky to me and I didn't think Ruby was buying it, either. How could a person recognise an omen from the many thousands of things he sees in one day?

But how do you know it's not just two black birds? I asked. *That maybe it just happened that way?*

Duke grinned and reached into his inside coat pocket and pulled something out. At first I thought it was a large wallet, but, when he gripped it tighter, I realised it was a hand gun. It looked like a .45. He pointed it straight at me and said, *Maybe this is an omen. What does it mean?*

He raised the gun and took aim at my head. He had a queer expression on his face, like he was enjoying himself immensely. I rocked backwards and rolled quickly to one side, desperate to get out of the line of fire. Suddenly, I found myself falling over the edge of the bank and into the river. It was so cold I almost screamed. I sank deeper and deeper into its icy currents. Water filled my ears and nose. I opened my eyes and could see only a rush of translucent green. Gasping for air, I kicked and stroked my way upwards.

When I finally surfaced, I could hear both Duke and Ruby laughing, and that idiot spouting something in his other language.

As I dried myself, I stared at them both and thought the only omen that Duke's gun represented was that he was a complete maniac. Ruby, however, was impressed, especially when he let her hold it, explaining where the safety catch was and how he loaded the bullets. Duke boasted that he'd stolen the gun from his uncle. He carried it to protect himself on the road, and to shoot rabbits and goannas whenever he ran out of food.

The clouds moved across the sun and I began shivering. I put the baby down for a nap in the van and began changing my wet clothes. I hadn't even pulled on a dry windcheater when Ruby called out, *We're going for a walk! See you later.*

I poked my head out the window and watched them stroll along the bank. As they chatted to one another, their arms waved in the air, like they were swatting flies.

They grew smaller and smaller and finally disappeared into the bush. And that is when I made my move, when I decided I would solve the mystery of Duke. His cricket bag was stashed behind the driver's seat. Careful not to wake the baby, I lifted it out, placed it on the ground by the fire, and pulled open the zip.

I don't know what I expected to find – more guns, maybe, or even a dagger. I pulled out a few pieces of clothing, a toothbrush and soap inside a plastic bag. There was a paperback novel called *Murder at No-Man's Creek* and a map of New South Wales that was so old the paper was torn along some of the creases. In one pocket was a penknife that opened into a fan of other instruments: a corkscrew, a bottle opener, a screwdriver, nail clippers. In another was a box of bullets. But, apart from that, there was nothing in the bag to prove Duke's identity or the real reason he was on the road. There was certainly no invitation to the Swedish Consulate, not even a Swedish vocabulary book. I didn't see any coins from when he'd been busking back in Maclean, and, the more I studied every item in the bag, the more suspicious I became. What was this kid on about and why was he so keen to travel with us? Again, I had that terrible thought that maybe he'd been set up by Roy to track us down, that our father had paid him off to lead us back to him. I became so obsessed with this idea that I just kept going through his stuff, over and over, as if by handling it I could divine the truth.

After about half an hour, I packed up all his things and returned the bag to the same spot behind the driver's seat. I thought it was dumb of Ruby to have wandered off with a boy she hardly knew, especially since he was carrying a gun. Hours passed and the sky filled with clouds the colour of charcoal. I sat with the baby beside the fire and studied our own map. I figured out we were about halfway between Grafton and Glen Innes, smack-bang in the middle of another national park. The isolation made me feel even more nervous, like when we'd been stuck on the logging track two days before, with no phone, no neighbours, no person to hear our cries if something went wrong.

Suddenly, a gunshot exploded in the distance, then another, and another, and my heart began hammering in my chest. I picked up the baby, ran to the van, and grabbed my air gun. I sat the baby in the back of the van, at the end of the built-in cupboards – the safest place I could think of. I knew an air gun was not much protection for us but at least I'd been able to shoot Roy in the eye and slow him down a little. And maybe, if I really concentrated, I could shoot Duke, too, wound him enough to wrestle away his gun and put a real bullet into his heart.

I sat crouching in the back with the barrel pointing out the open side window, my finger cocked on the trigger. I waited five, maybe ten, minutes, imagining Ruby dead in some gully after being raped or tortured. I imagined blowing Duke's brains out in revenge, and all his insides splattering across the grass. But, after a few more minutes, I saw him and Ruby round a bend in the river. I could see Duke was carrying some kind of dead animal, and that he and Ruby were holding hands. As they approached the van, both grinning widely, I knew instantly that they'd been in the woods, fucking.

I recognised the look because I could always tell when my parents had had sex. I'd come home from school and Roy would be calm, sitting on the porch, sipping a beer, with a half-smile on his face as he stared out at the horizon. And, as my mother moved around the kitchen, making tea, I would kiss her, and she would taste different to me. I didn't so much smell Roy on her lips as something salty and slightly chemical, like how I imagined the sea would taste. Even she would have a peaceful, dreamy expression on her face as she boiled water and buttered toast.

As Duke and Ruby drew closer, I recognised exactly the same look on Duke's face, as if all his problems had been drained by that single act. He was bouncing along, swinging a dead rabbit in one hand. But, when I squinted and studied Ruby's face, I could see that she was frowning and tightly smiling at the same time, as if she was faking her own happiness. I put down my air gun, picked up the baby, and crawled out of the van.

Well, Mark, announced Ruby. *We've got it all worked out.* She still had dead leaves and twigs in her hair and on her sleeves. I couldn't believe she could do it with someone she hardly even knew.

We're an hour or so from Glen Innes, she continued, picking a thistle off her jumper. Duke dropped the rabbit beside the fire and sat down.

So? I said, wondering where this was going.

You've got a rich uncle there, right? said Duke. He was stroking the rabbit's head and fingering the bloody gunshot wound.

I didn't like where this was going, and shifted the baby from one hip to the other. *We hardly know him.*

That's not the point, said Duke. *In some ways, it makes it better.*

Makes what better?

Ruby and Duke exchanged looks. I could tell they'd shared a lot more than bodily fluids that day.

Well, he cheated your father out of his inheritance, said Duke. *That's got to make him feel just a little bit guilty. We're going to sting him for some money.*

We're supposed to be going to Sydney – I was getting more and more angry – *to find our Aunty Candy.*

Don't get your dick in a twist, said Ruby. *We are going to Sydney. And Duke's going on to Melbourne.*

So, then why –

Don't you want to have a bit of fun? she continued. *After all we've been through? Don't you want to eat in a restaurant, buy some new clothes, stay in a nice motel?*

I sighed and put the baby on the ground. *You two just want a bed to fuck in.*

Ruby suddenly rushed forward and slapped me hard on the cheek. *You know fuck all, Mark! You don't know anything!*

Yeah, well I know one thing, I said. *Your boyfriend here's a phony. A big, fat phony!*

What the fuck are you –

He's not going to Melbourne. He doesn't speak Swedish. And he's not going off to meet that bloody King and Queen.

Duke jumped to his feet. *I am so. On the twenty-fourth of this month.*

Bullshit! I said, turning back to Ruby. *He reckons he's got an invitation. Have you seen it? Has he shown it to you?*

Ruby frowned and glanced warily at Duke. *I went through his bag,* I added. *There's no invite, no Swedish books, not even a map of Victoria. He's using us, Ruby. He's a fake.*

Duke's face was crimson. He began unzipping his jacket. I wasn't sure if he was reaching for his gun or removing the jacket so he could punch me out. I ducked sideways, but Ruby stood her ground. I watched him reach into his inside pocket and pull out a piece of paper. He unfolded it and handed it to Ruby. She looked at it and held it up to me. I crept forward and took it from her.

The paper read:

The Consular General of Sweden, Ove Andersson
cordially invites
Duke Doyle
to a gala reception to celebrate the royal visit of
His Majesty King Carl XVI Gustaf
and
Her Majesty Queen Silvia of Sweden
2 pm, 24 June
Consulate of Sweden
21 St Georges Rd,
Toorak, Victoria, 3142
R.S.V.P. by 15 June: (03) 9827-4224
Dress: Lounge suit
Valet parking available

I handed the invitation back to Duke, who was smirking. I felt like a real dickhead.

Even though Duke had proven he wasn't a phony or a cheat, I still felt their plan was a big mistake. Oh sure, even though I liked the idea of staying in beachside motels – I'd never been on a proper holiday before – and eating fresh seafood, I thought it was too risky to look up our uncle and ask him for some money.

What if Roy's there already? I asked. *You said so yourself that he might drive to Bob's.*

That was days ago, Mark, said Ruby. *And anyway, they hate each other.*

We've already got that covered, boasted Duke, as he sat on the ground, skinning the rabbit.

Oh yeah? I folded my arms. *How?*

We'll park around the corner from Bob's place, said Ruby. *And Duke here is going to go up to the front door and knock on it.*

Duke worked the blade underneath the fur of the rabbit's belly and began peeling it back. It sounded like he was pulling two pieces of Velcro apart. *I'm going to pretend my grandfather built the house and ask permission to come in and have a look around.* He paused and grinned. *I'll know straight away if Roy's there or not. It's not like I could miss a one-legged man.*

If Roy wasn't there, they explained, the next part of the plan was to wait a while and then have me and the baby knock on the door.

I was supposed to tell Uncle Bob that Roy, the baby, and I were passing through town, on our way back home. I was to say Roy was in a pub downtown, getting drunk. Then I was to start crying and, after my uncle invited me inside, I would tell him the baby and I hadn't eaten in two days, that we'd run out of petrol and were virtually broke. And basically I was supposed to carry on like that until he felt so sorry for me he'd give me some cash and send me on my way, just to get rid of me.

Why do I have to do it? I asked. *Why not you?*

Ruby rolled her eyes. *You're younger and more innocent, dummy. And he'll feel sorry for the baby.*

I didn't want to do it. I still thought Duke was using us in some way, that he had some sort of agenda apart from getting himself to Melbourne. Ruby and I were taking all the risks – not him. But after my outburst about Duke being a fake, I felt foolish. And then, as he sat there merrily gutting the rabbit, he glanced at me, smirking, and said, *Catch any more fish?* And that was the final straw. I resolved that I would prove to my sister that I was just as clever as him.

We didn't have enough petrol to get us all the way to Glen Innes. Night fell and, after we ate most of the charred rabbit, Ruby handed the plastic container and the hose to Duke and told him to siphon some tractor fuel from the farm over the hill. Duke obediently jumped to his feet. It was as if they'd worked out this secret deal, as if Ruby could ask anything of him now that she'd allowed him inside her.

Hang on, I said. *That's my job.*

OK, said Duke, handing me the container. *But I'll walk over with you and show you where to go.*

We set off together along a track that wound up a gentle rise. It was cold and slightly misty, and for some reason every little rustle and crunch in the forest made me jump. The beam of the torch wavered ahead of us like a weak theatre spotlight, shining on rocks and ferns and the corpse of a lizard. The moon moved between clouds, as if it were shadowing us. And then, out of the blue, Duke asked me a question that unnerved me even more.

Do you know how your father lost his leg?

We rounded a bend and the track narrowed, forcing us to walk closer together. *No,* I said. *Nobody knows.* I glanced at Duke in the pale light. I thought I saw him smile.

I know, he boasted.

Bull, I replied, a little too quickly. *Not even Mum knew.*

If you say so, he said, in a teasing, sing-song way. We walked on in silence, but I couldn't get Duke's smarmy voice out of my head.

Don't believe everything my sister tells you, I added. *When it comes to bullshit, Ruby's a true artist.*

We reached the crest of the hill and stopped. The air seemed even colder up there. I could see the outline of a large, old-fashioned house in the middle of a paddock, with a wide, wrap-around veranda. Most of the downstairs windows were glowing with light.

Ruby was living at home when it happened, he said, still in that sing-song voice. *Weren't you in foster care?*

By this time, I wanted to snatch the torch out of his hand and smash him over the head with it. *Shut up, Duke. If Ruby knew how it happened, she would've told me.*

I started walking ahead of him, towards the house. The plateau had been cleared of trees, except for a couple out the back, beside the barn.

How can you be so sure? said Duke.

Everyone back in town has their own story about Roy. I've heard so many, I could write a book about it. What difference does it make, anyway?

Duke shrugged.

He finally shut up and led me to the barn. The door was wide open, as if someone had been expecting us. Sacks of feed were stacked in high columns along one wall. There were ten-gallon drums and broken bits of machinery on the cement floor. The whole place stank of petrol and manure.

The tractor was parked at the other end. I removed the fuel cap, inserted the hose, and went to work, while Duke stood beside me, holding the torch. I sucked for what seemed like a long time – and for a while I thought the tank was empty of petrol, but I kept drawing and drawing until the first spurt of burning liquid scorched my mouth.

I spat out and pushed the end of the hose into the plastic container, just as Ruby had taught me. I was feeling pleased with myself for having accomplished this one feat, in front of Duke, without making a single mistake. We stood beside one another, watching the container slowly fill.

Duke switched the torch from one hand to the other and said in a low voice, *So you believe that story about the gangrene, do you?*

I kept my eyes on the container and ignored him.

Or that he fell off a moving train carriage?

I was so mad my fists were balled inside my coat pockets. *Cut it out, Duke.*

Or that he cut off his own leg?

I said, SHUT UP.

Do you think he could do that? Do you? You want to know the truth?

Before I could stop myself, I took a step back and punched him hard in the face. He howled briefly, dropped the torch, and went toppling backwards, into an empty oil drum that crashed to the floor and went rolling across the barn. Suddenly one, then two dogs started barking.

I made a grab for the torch, but Duke snatched it up first and jumped to his feet. With his free hand, he rubbed his jaw. *What'd you do that for, you stupid fuck?* The barking was growing louder. I heard a screen door slam. I felt so panicky I couldn't think properly. The next thing I saw was Duke grabbing the container of fuel and running towards the door.

We'll have to split up, he called. And then he vanished into the night.

By the time I was outside, I could see a man with a torch hurrying across the grass, two big dogs leaping and barking at his side. Duke had turned his own torch off and I couldn't tell which way he'd headed. I ran behind the barn and went in the opposite direction from the path we'd been on earlier, across what looked like a paddock. I could hear cows scattering ahead of me, the dull thud of their hooves against the ground. When I looked behind me, I glimpsed the farmer disappearing into the barn. Then I heard him shout something and, before I knew it, the barking began growing louder and louder and I realised the dogs were not far behind me.

I pushed myself to run faster, even though, because it was so dark, I had no idea where I was going. Suddenly, I tripped on something – a rock, maybe – and stumbled, falling hard on my side and grazing my right hand. I scrambled to my feet and fled. The dogs were almost upon me now. The ground rose upwards and, in the faint moonlight, I glimpsed the edge of the forest rushing towards me, an outline of trees against the sky. I couldn't see a track or trail, so I just hurtled straight into the bush, into branches and hanging vines, damp foliage and spider webs. I could hear the dogs howling and leaping behind me, struggling through the thick undergrowth. And then I ran smack-bang into a tree trunk and bounced backwards, a terrible pain piercing my head.

But, by the time the dogs were lunging at me, I was shinnying up that tree and onto one of its boughs. One of the beasts was nipping at my feet and bit a chunk of flesh from my ankle.

I don't know how long I stayed up there, rubbing my sore head – all I know is that it seemed like a long time. The dogs continued to bark as they circled the tree, sometimes leaping on their hind legs against the trunk. I took off my shoe and one of my socks and wrapped it twice around my ankle to stem the bleeding. I was scared the farmer would follow the sound of his dogs and would appear at any moment.

I remembered I had a packet of Cheezels in my pocket. And that was how I managed to calm the mutts down, by tossing the snacks on to the ground, one by one, like I was feeding a flock of birds. I could hear their crunching and slobbering in the dark. By the time they'd finished, they were quiet and only occasionally whined for more. After a while, they must have grown bored waiting for more food and wandered back in the direction of the house.

The moon shone through a cloud veined with deep

purple and grey. Nearby, frogs chorused. I couldn't blame Duke for deserting me like that – I probably would have done the same thing if I'd been in his shoes – but I was mad at him for banging on about Roy and how he'd lost his leg. Duke hadn't even met Roy, and I resented the fact that he pretended to know more about my own father than I did. As I sat there listening to the frog, I realised that he'd teased me on purpose, that he'd deliberately wound me up so I would lose my temper and make a mistake during the siphoning. He was more cunning than I'd realised, and I wondered if he was trying to drive a wedge between me and Ruby so he could have her all to himself.

Well, I thought, when we get to Glen Innes, I'll show him. I'll show them both. I'll con so much money out of Uncle Bob that we'll be able to afford to hire a limo and a chauffeur to drive us all the way to Sydney.

More and more rhythmic croaking filled the night and I found myself wishing that my mother had loved frogs. If she had loved frogs, then maybe their song would have been an omen, a sign that she was here right now, trying to communicate with me. She hadn't particularly liked dogs, either. Or bush walking at night. In fact, there was nothing around me to indicate her presence – or the fact that she had any kind of existence beyond her death. And that got me thinking about how I would recognise her if she did in fact try to speak to me through a sign. What would it be? And how would I know it was her? I made a mental catalogue of the things she loved: 4711 Eau de Cologne, Chinese silk wraps, the smell of freshly cut grass, salami, the colour turquoise. And then her favourite – the first star in the evening sky.

When I thought that the dogs and the farmer had retreated and that it was safe, I climbed down the tree and tried to find my way back to the campsite. My ankle was sore and it was hard to see in the darkness. I made it to the farm without too much trouble, but my face and hands were cut and scratched from stumbling through the bush. I glanced over at the house, and all but one of the upstairs lights had been switched off. Still wary of the dogs, I kept on the edge of the cleared paddock and traced it around to the place where I figured the trail to our campsite began. I walked back and forth, over and over, but each narrow opening in the forest led me nowhere, just straight into a thicket of trees or a great slab of rock. Each time, I'd return to the clearing and try again, until, at one point, I couldn't make my way back to the clearing and found myself trapped amidst a web of vines and branches. No matter which way I turned, there seemed to be no way out, as if the bush had closed around me. I hadn't felt such panic since I'd discovered the corpse of my mother and, for a long while, as I clawed my way through the deep foliage, trying to find a path, I imagined someone, days later, discovering my own corpse, half-buried in damp leaves and ferns, with maggots crawling out of my nose and ears.

I was gripped by this fear for what seemed like a long time – it was an eternity being lost in the bush that night – until I saw a beam of light flickering faintly through the undergrowth and recognised my sister's voice calling me.

Ruby took me by the arm and led me back to the track that wound down to the camp, as if I were blind. She talked to me gently and kept asking me if I was all right. I don't know if Duke had told her exactly what had happened between us earlier, but I was surprised by how nice Ruby was behaving towards me, like we were the best of friends again.

Back at camp, she sat me by the dwindling fire and bathed my ankle. I told her how the dogs had chased me, how I'd escaped into the boughs of a tree, and then how I'd become lost in the bush. Through all this, Duke sat in the front of the van, playing with the baby, pretending not to be the least bit interested in what I had to say, but I could tell that he was listening closely. I suspected he was worried I'd tell Ruby what he'd said about Roy, that she'd bawl him out for being such a lying shithead.

Well, said Ruby. *Poor Duke turned up here with a black eye. Tripped over a log. At least he didn't spill the petrol.*

Tripped over a log, eh? I said, in that mocking, sing-song voice he'd used on me earlier. He obviously didn't have the guts to tell Ruby the truth. And it was then that I sensed I had something over him: he was a coward and a liar and he knew that I knew it. And this realisation lifted a weight from my shoulders. The little bastard and I now shared a secret.

Soon we were back on the trail, heading towards Glen Innes. Ruby was behind the wheel and Duke sat beside her in the front seat. I stayed in the back with the baby. It was after midnight and I noticed through the window that a cluster of stars had appeared in the sky.

The track had so many sharp bends that Ruby didn't talk at all, just concentrated on her driving. Even Duke was unusually quiet as he leaned back and rested his feet on the dashboard. My ankle throbbed and my skin was stinging with scratches and cuts, but I didn't really mind any more. In the rear-view mirror, I'd seen the kisser I'd given Duke – the purplish bruise darkening around his eye – and for some reason it made me feel happy, happier than I'd been in months.

The baby and I dozed for a while, lulled by the rhythm of the tyres against the track. I woke just after we hit the Gwydir Highway. I saw a road sign that said Bald Knob and snorted to myself. *Hey, Duke*, I joked, *I didn't know they'd named this town after you.* Ruby laughed and nudged him. Duke remained silent and shifted in his seat. I could tell now that I was getting under his skin, and, once I'd conned a large sum of cash out of Uncle Bob, there'd be no way he'd try to push me around again.

We reached Glen Innes before dawn. Great clouds of mist rolled down the main street. Ruby had to slow down to a crawl to avoid hitting anything. From what I could see, it was another old-fashioned town: sturdy brick buildings and a wooden pub with a wide, second-floor veranda. It was freezing inside the van and Ruby cranked up the heat.

Duke finally broke his silence and asked, *So what does this uncle do?*

Ruby shrugged. *I don't think he does anything.*

He must do something, said Duke. *I'm just trying to figure out what time he'd get up — when he'd leave the house.*

I know he's married. Ruby made a right-hand turn. We passed an old corner pub with stained-glass windows. *No kids, but. I think it's her problem. Maybe they're not doing it right.*

Investments, I piped up.

What? asked Duke.

Roy told me he lives off the stock market. Puts his money in rubber bands or some bloody thing.

A Rubber Band Baron! Duke laughed. *And I thought my family was crazy.*

Ahead of us was a cheap-looking motel, with a rectangle of brick, single-storey suites with all the doors facing on to a bitumen car park. A VACANCY sign flashed red in the dawn light.

Turn in here, said Duke, pointing to the driveway.

What for? asked Ruby.

Duke pulled his feet down from the dashboard. *I'll show you an old trick me and Honey used to pull.*

I could tell Ruby was already in competition with this girl from Duke's past, that anything Honey had done, she would do better. It was like being jealous of a ghost or someone who only existed as a character in a book, and as she swung the van into the drive, past the closed reception office, I was surprised that someone as tough as Ruby would allow a boy to influence her so much.

About a dozen cars were parked alongside each other, right in front of the motel-room doors. Ruby pulled up in one of the empty spaces and turned off the ignition. I thought Duke was going to try to break into a vehicle – steal one, perhaps, or steal something from one. He was always boasting about pinching cars and I figured that maybe after I'd given him a black eye he wanted to prove himself.

But he jumped out of the van and headed for the furthest empty parking space, right at the end of the row. There was a bluish tinge to the dawn light and mist curled around him in long, wispy tendrils. I had a sudden fantasy about Ruby quickly reversing and us taking off together by ourselves again, leaving Duke behind with nothing more than his gun and his invitation to meet the King and Queen of Sweden.

We watched him turn and head for one of the motel-room doors. He put his hand on the knob, turned it, and then moved on to the next one. He tried that door, too, and the next, and the next, working his way towards us. He skipped any room that had a car parked in front of it. I thought it was a stupid exercise, and told Ruby so, but, right after I said that, a door magically opened – the one directly in front of us. Duke raised his hand theatrically, and bowed to us, like he'd just made a woman vanish. I could have thumped him in his good eye for acting so superior.

People check out early, he explained, after he'd opened the side door and grabbed his cricket bag. *They drop the keys in the box at Reception but don't bother to lock the door.*

You're a genius, Duke! said Ruby. She jumped out of the van and I followed with the baby, who was still asleep.

I'd never been inside a hotel or motel room and didn't know what to expect. Oh, I'd seen them in movies – all plush carpet, chandeliers and ice buckets of champagne. Of course, I wasn't assuming a dump of a motel in Glen Innes could match Hollywood in any way, but I was pretty disappointed by how shabby it was: dark brick walls, a sagging venetian blind, a bench made out of plasterboard. The beige carpet was stained dark brown in some places. The queen-sized bed was a mess of sheets and blankets; on the side table, an ashtray brimmed with butts.

Welcome to the Ritz, I murmured, looking around.

It's better than that stinking van. Duke walked over to the air conditioner and turned the heat on.

I put the baby down on the bed between two pillows and covered her with a blanket while Ruby raided the bar fridge. She pulled out a couple of chocolate bars, some small bottles of juice, and three stubbies of VB. On top of the fridge was a small basket, holding a packet of peanuts, a half-bottle of red wine, sachets of coffee and sugar, and several tea bags.

Cool! said Ruby. *Let's have brekky.* She began boiling some water in the jug. I found the remote and turned on the TV. I flicked channels until I came across the early-morning news. I was half-hoping there'd be a bulletin about some runaway kid with a gun hitchhiking down the coast, with a picture of Duke flashing across the screen, or maybe even a story about me, Ruby and the baby and how we'd disappeared. But the presenter just droned on about the price of wool and the floods on the Northern Tablelands. For a while it made me feel heavy and sad that no one loved or cared enough to report any of us missing – not even Duke's aunt and uncle, not even our own father. And certainly not Duke's mother, who'd deserted him two years before.

In between cups of coffee, we took it in turns to take a shower. After being on the road for five nights, it felt like a luxury. Steam fogged the mirror as I washed and conditioned my hair, and after that I just stood there for a long time, allowing the jets of hot water to pummel my back. When the baby woke up, we bathed her, too. She kept grabbing the soap and trying to chew it. For breakfast she drank half a cup of milk, then nestled back with a pillow on the floor and watched cartoons on TV.

Duke cracked open a bottle of VB and took a few gulps without taking a breath.

He left the bottle on the bench before following Ruby into the bathroom and closing the door. One of the taps squeaked and the shower began running again. I could hear Ruby giggling, a muffled phrase from Duke, and I could already imagine what they were doing in there.

I found a local telephone book in one of the bedside drawers and looked up the name Robert Stamp. There were three Stamps listed for Glen Innes, but only one was prefaced by the initial 'R'. He was listed as living at 924 Grey Street. I wrote down the address and telephone number.

By now, steam was drifting beneath the bathroom door and rising into the air. Duke was making a weird sound, almost like a growling dog, but Ruby was curiously quiet. Maybe I should have covered my ears or stepped outside but the longer I heard Duke's grunting and sighing, the more I couldn't stop listening. Somehow, my growing disgust with him was becoming pleasurable, as in the way self-inflicted pain can provide a kind of relief, like picking at a scab or pulling out an aching tooth. I walked across to the bench and pulled down my pants. As Duke's groaning rose into a breathy wail, I picked up his half-finished bottle of VB, stuck my cock into the opening, and began pissing. I watched the beer froth and swirl until foam bubbled up and tickled my knob.

The shower suddenly stopped running. I set the beer back on the bench, zipped myself up, and rushed back to the bed.

The bathroom door opened and a cloud of steam billowed out. Ruby giggled and boasted to Duke: *I bet Honey couldn't do that.*

She walked into the the bedroom, wearing his T-shirt, her wet hair turbaned in a white towel, and Duke followed, wearing only his underpants. They both seemed relaxed yet smug, as if they shared an exquisite secret.

Duke picked up the beer and took a swig. I sat there, rigid, waiting to see if he would taste the difference, preparing myself to run or fight or throw an ashtray at him when he realised what I'd done.

But the idiot just grinned and burped and took another sip, and I had to tighten all the muscles in my body and stare at the TV to stop myself from laughing.

I waited a few minutes, until I'd calmed down, before I spoke again. *Hey, Ruby,* I said, holding up the piece of paper. *I've already got Uncle Bob's address.*

I handed it to her and she glanced at it. *Good work, Sherlock. Now we just have to get directions.* Then, before I could stop her, she snatched the beer from Duke and took a swig. I watched with horror as she rolled it around her mouth briefly, then swallowed. I was hoping that she'd be just as distracted as Duke, that she wouldn't notice the difference. But as the taste of the tainted beer hit her, I saw her expression change from contentment to suspicion.

She held up the bottle, eyed it, and then flashed me a furious, knowing look. I stood my ground, smirking, daring her to retaliate. I thought she'd throw the bottle at me, but all she did was set it down on the bench and cross her arms.

Go and get some nappies, Mark, she said quietly.

I knew what she was up to – she wanted to get rid of me so she could fuck Duke again, but this time in a proper bed with sheets and pillows.

Why don't you?

She snatched up the beer and, before I could duck, splashed some in my face. *Fuckin' get 'em.*

I wiped my eyes and backed away.

She hurled some more beer at me. *This room stinks of piss.*

I haven't got any money, I said.

She pointed the top of the bottle at my stomach. *Lift them.*

If I get caught, it'll stuff up our sting on Uncle Bob, I pleaded. *We'll never get to Sydney.*

Duke sighed and pulled out his wallet. *Here,* he said, and palmed me a twenty-dollar note. *It's all I've got left. So bring back the change.*

I had no more excuses, so I took the money. *When I get back, we should clear out of here, before the owners open the office.* And then, as I walked out the door, I couldn't resist looking back and saying, *Hey, Duke, there's more beer in the fridge.*

On the street, it was so cold that the wind stung my face. I walked up and down the main street for a while. There was nothing open but a run-down milk bar. The mist was lifting and a few cars slowly rattled down the road. I thought about our uncle and, if I was to run into him, whether I'd be able to recognise his face. I hadn't seen him since I was about six years old, when he called in to see us on his way to Far North Queensland. I couldn't remember much about him except the strong, tart smell of his aftershave and how I could gaze down at his black polished boots and see my reflection in the leather.

A convenience store finally opened. I bought a packet of Huggies with Duke's money and swiped a Violet Crumble bar for myself. As I was heading back to the motel, I realised the main street I was walking on was in fact Grey Street, the one our uncle lived on. I figured that, unless he lived in a shop or a pub, his house must be further out of town.

I rounded the corner and headed towards the blinking VACANCY sign. I slipped past Reception, which was still closed. The sky was heavy with rain clouds and I was expecting it to start pouring again at any moment. As I crossed the car park, I realised I couldn't remember which room we were in – all the doors were the same. I glanced over towards the remaining vehicles, looking for our van. But it had completely vanished.

My heart raced as I scanned the other cars, as if a second check could somehow make it reappear. By this time, I wasn't thinking straight and rushed over to the general area where I thought Ruby had parked. Frantic, I tried one doorknob after another until I came to a door that was half-open. I pushed on it gingerly and peered inside. It looked like the room we'd all been in earlier – the same TV and plasterboard bench, the mini-bar and blinds – but I suspected they were all identical. It wasn't until I spotted a shitty nappy on the floor that I realised Ruby and Duke had cleared off, taking along the baby, leaving me with nothing but a packet of Huggies and a little over seven dollars.

6

Not even his wife, Sapphire, knew what was really going on. Oh, she might have suspected something — the odd truck-stop whore when he was on the road — but nothing too serious or complicated.

Of course, there's been a lot of things said around the traps about Roy Stamp and our cousin, Tanya. Everyone knows that Tanya used to go out with one of Roy's co-workers, a bloke named Sparrow. They were real close — Sparrow had even proposed — but Tanya dumped Sparrow once she met Roy. There's this idea floating around that Sparrow was so gutted by being dumped that he tried to kill Roy for stealing her away from him. But we're related to the person who attacked him, and we're the only ones who have the real goods on old Stampy, who know the reason he came to be separated from that limb.

Roy had been seeing our Tanya for a few months. She was a bit older than him and lived in a fibro house around the corner from his Tenterfield depot. She had a bunch of kids, but they'd been taken off her after one of them accidentally drank her methadone and was hospitalised. We tried to adopt them but DOCS wouldn't let us.

Tenterfield is only half an hour away from Roy's hometown in Queensland, just over the border, and he was in and out of here several times a week. It wasn't hard for him to hide the affair from Sapphire. At first, he'd slip Tanya some money for her trouble, a little something to help her with the rent or to pass on to us — she owes us heaps — and for a while this worked out well for them both and Tanya was able to put a down-payment on an '83 Holden. But, as time went on, she became more demanding, wanting to be taken out to the bowling club, to be wined and dined in restaurants. She even started pestering him to leave his wife and kids, and what started out as a simple agreement between two adults turned out to be something far more messy and complex. The reason he started seeing Tanya in the first place was to get away from a nagging woman and have a little fun. And here it was, happening all over again — a harmless distraction turning into one big pain in the arse. And so, instead of doing the sensible thing and ending it with Tanya right then and there, Roy decides to complicate his life even more: he takes up with a truck-stop cashier in her early twenties and begins cheating on his mistress.

The cashier, Halo, lived and worked about fifteen minutes out of town. Roy never gave her money, but she had a taste for speed, and Roy, being a truckie, had a regular supply. It didn't go on for long — maybe two or three weeks; not long enough for it to be anything serious. Occasionally they went disco-dancing at The Emporium — she was a big ABBA fan — but most of the time they'd get high and watch late-night television in bed.

On the morning of New Year's Day, they were dozing off when a car pulled into the drive. Roy stirred and went to get up, but Halo, who was still half-asleep, said, Don't worry. It's just my mum. *Apparently, the mother was having a barbeque that day and had turned up to borrow a punch bowl and a set of steak knives. Roy turned over and fell back asleep. The bedroom door was open.*

No one knows exactly how much time passed between Roy nodding off and what happened next. All we know for sure is that when Roy jolted awake, the blade was already slicing into him. He felt a fork of pain in his leg and, before he realised what was happening, she was stabbing him again in the calf. By then, Halo was screaming at her to stop. Roy grabbed the mother's wrist and was wrestling the carving knife away from her. This all happened in maybe six or seven seconds, so fast he couldn't have taken in everything at once. It was only after he got hold of the knife, and the mother screamed, You bastard! *that he recognised her voice. It was Tanya, all wide-eyed and crazy and covered in blood. She'd never told Roy about her grown-up daughter because she thought that particular piece of information would've aged her too much.*

Well, that's how Roy Stamp lost two mistresses and one leg. Tanya didn't exactly amputate it or anything – in fact, we all think she was aiming for a different part of his anatomy. But Tanya had carved him up pretty well, and yet he refused to go to the hospital or even see a doctor. He didn't want to have to explain how it happened, didn't want people talking and the gossip getting back to Sapphire. He just wrapped his wounds in bandages and told his wife and everyone else he'd been attacked by a pit bull, which in some ways was the truth. A few weeks passed and his leg became infected, and still he wouldn't get help. By the end of January, he could barely walk. By the time Sapphire drove him to Tenterfield Base Hospital in February, his foot and calf were so

black with gangrene there was nothing the doctors could do but
pump him with antibiotics and cut off his limb.

We never knew Tanya had it in her; since then, she's become a
legend in our part of the world. She was the one who told us all
this, after she got out of rehab, and after she disowned her grown-
up daughter and came to live with us. Not only did Roy lose his
leg, he lost his job, as well. All that in the same year that Sapphire
had another baby. We're all amazed he had the time and energy to
get her pregnant, with two mistresses and all.

When she's drunk, Tanya still tells everyone that she should
have aimed a little higher.

It was hard for me to believe that Ruby had dumped me on
purpose, that she and Duke had conspired from the
beginning to leave me stranded in Glen Innes. But all the
evidence pointed to that conclusion – there was no note, no
money left, no sign to reveal where they'd gone. Ruby and
I had fought throughout our childhood, had even been
cruel to one another, but probably no more than the
average brother and sister and, after losing our mother and
all that we'd been through together, it just didn't make
sense that she'd abandon me so easily.

Perhaps her infatuation with Duke had clouded her
judgment. I'd heard that women didn't think straight when
they were in love, like the way our mother used to return to
Roy, over and over, to cop another belting. When I was in
foster care, the teenage daughter of my substitute parents
ran away with her married history teacher and lived with

him in secret for three months. The police eventually found her locked in a cupboard of the farmhouse the man had rented. When they opened the doors and told her she was free, she said she'd prefer to stay in the cupboard rather than go home to her family.

I didn't think Ruby was as nutty as that, no matter how much she'd fallen for Duke. Maybe after I'd left the hotel room, he'd threatened her. Maybe he'd pulled his gun, said he'd shoot her and the baby if she didn't follow his directions. I wouldn't have put it past him. He'd been dying to get me out of the picture from the moment he'd first clapped eyes on Ruby. That way he could have more sex. I decided he was a bully, like Roy. I remembered Aunty Candy once saying, *All girls fall in love with a replica of their fathers*, and, as I stood there gazing at the empty motel room, it was the first time that her statement had ever made sense to me.

I really didn't know what to do next, but I was aware of the fact that I had virtually no money. I backtracked across the car park and returned to the convenience store. As I entered I put on a sorry face, like I'd just been crying or something, and told the middle-aged woman behind the counter that I'd bought the wrong brand of disposable nappies, and that my mother had yelled at me for being so stupid.

What brand does she want, love? The woman had purple upswept hair that made it seem as if a tower of fairy floss stood on top of her head.

Snuggies, I replied, rubbing one eye.

Snuggies ... she said. *I don't think we stock that brand.*

Of course they didn't stock that brand because no such brand existed.

I've got to get Snuggies, I pleaded. *She'll belt me if I don't.* I held the packet of Huggies out to her as if it stank badly, or was a bomb that was about to blow up.

All right, sweetheart. Don't you fret. She took the nappies from me, pressed No Sale on the cash register and gave me back my twelve dollars and seventy-five cents. *Try Kmart down the road. They stock everything.*

Other stores were opening by now. I didn't want to spend any money on things I could steal, so I kept Duke's change tight in my pocket. I wondered if Duke and Ruby were going through with their plan to rip off Uncle Bob, or if that had just been an excuse to get rid of me. I looked up at the street number above the doorway of a shop called Myrtle's Tea Room. It was number eighty-four. The numbers increased as I kept walking. I figured if I stayed on Grey Street and headed in the direction I was going, in about ten or so minutes I would be close to my uncle's house and possibly the sister who had deserted me. Failing that, I resolved to get to Sydney as fast as I could, either by hitchhiking or sneaking on to a passenger train.

I crossed the main intersection and the next block was lined with single-level fibro houses bleached almost colourless by the sun. They either had chainlink fences or no fences at all, and carports with rusting beams. If this is where our uncle lives, I thought, he'd either blown all his money or the stories about him ripping off Roy's inheritance were a pack of lies. Either way, the likelihood of stinging Bob for some cash diminished with my every step. But I reasoned to myself that nothing could be as bad as that final image of my mother, that no person or thing could wound me more than my own past.

I reached a corner and a rush of wind cut through me. Shivering, I zipped up my jacket and shoved my fists into my pockets. I was just stepping down from the kerb, about to cross the road, when I heard a horn honking behind me. I didn't pay any attention. I wanted to get to the other side and out of the freezing wind as soon as possible. But the beep-beep-beep continued, and, as I stepped up on to the footpath, I glanced sideways to see the van pulling up beside me. My sister leaned out of the driver's window. *Where the fuck have you been, Mark?* she barked. *Hurry up and get in!*

I was so glad to see her that I did as I was told. I'd never been happier to crawl back into that familiar stink of mould and shitty nappies.

Instead of driving on to Uncle Bob's, Ruby backed up and detoured down the next side street. Duke was in the passenger seat, bouncing the baby on his knee. *What happened to you?* I demanded. *When I got back, you were gone!*

Well, if you didn't have to take so long, Ruby snapped. We turned left at the first corner. One of the cupboard doors swung open and hit me on the back of the head.

It's not his fault, said Duke. I was surprised he was defending me and wondered what he was up to. He turned around in his seat and faced me. *Soon after you left, the boss's wife walked in to clean up the room. When she found us there, eating all the food and drinking the beer, she hit the roof. Started yelling and threatening to call the cops. What else could we do? When she went to get her husband, we had to clear out right away.*

I closed the cupboard door and rubbed the back of my head. *You could have looked for me*, I said. *I was only around the corner.*

What the bloody hell do you think we've been doing? said Ruby. *Taking a holiday?*

In fact, that's exactly what I thought they'd been doing – pissing off on a holiday without me.

So, said Duke, *did you get the nappies?*

No, I lied, *there was nothing open.*

Ruby turned left again and pulled up in front of a vacant lot. By this time, I was enjoying myself and the idea of riling Duke.

I'd give you your money back, I added, *but I don't have it any more.*

What the hell? he said. *What did you –*

When I got back to the motel room, that woman was still there. But she had her husband, too. I had to give them the twenty to pay for the food and beer. Otherwise, they were calling the cops.

Duke rolled his eyes and sighed, but there was nothing he could do. I gripped the paper money and coins in my pocket and secretly congratulated myself for my quick thinking. I'd finally conned the con artist.

Well, said Ruby, *we'll just have to go to work on Uncle Bob.*

The way I figure it, number 924 Grey Street is just around the corner. Ready to go to work, Duke?

He nodded and passed me over the baby, who was grinning widely, as if she understood what we were up to and thought it was hilarious. Ruby grilled Duke about what he was supposed to do and say when he arrived on Bob's doorstep, about his grandfather having built number 924, about wanting to see the interior of the house. He was also instructed to keep his eyes peeled for Roy's red-and-white Fairlane, Queensland number plate 694 YUB. All this, Duke repeated back to her, as if he was at school, learning his times tables by rote.

Finally he kissed Ruby on the lips and gave me one of his exaggerated salutes. Then he disappeared into the morning's grey weather.

While Duke was gone, Ruby quizzed me on how I should act and what I was supposed to say when I met Uncle Bob. As the baby wriggled in my arms, we went over the routine again and again, like two criminals trying to get their story straight before an interrogation. If he asked me about our mother, I was to pretend that she wasn't dead, that she was very much alive and well, back at home. If Bob or his wife offered to drive me and the baby back to the pub in town where Roy was supposed to be drinking, I was to thank them politely and say no. I would have to explain that Roy would kick my arse for looking them up and begging for a handout.

By the time Ruby and I had nailed every detail and my responses to each possible question or mishap, about three-quarters of an hour must have passed. I didn't like to worry but it seemed as if Duke had been gone a long time, considering it would take only a few minutes to look through Uncle Bob's house.

Perhaps they're having tea, joked Ruby, resting her elbows on the steering wheel.

Thunder rumbled across the sky. The baby fell asleep in my arms. I put her down on the mattress and covered her with blankets. Fat raindrops began splattering the windscreen. I had this idea that maybe Duke had struck out on his own, that he'd grown bored with Ruby and was hitchhiking down the highway, or that he was heading towards the next town where he'd walk on his hands for money.

Shit, said Ruby, after about another fifteen or so minutes. *What the fuck is he doing in there?*

Don't worry, I said, trying to convince myself. *At least he's got a gun.*

After a few more minutes, she punched the dashboard. *I can't stand it any more*, she said. *Go and have a look through the window. See what he's up to.*

Of course, I was curious, but I was scared about what my perving might reveal. *Why don't you?* I said. *I'll watch the baby.*

Ruby sighed and shook her head. *You can't drive. If we get into trouble, I need to be behind the wheel. I'll need to get us out of here.*

Of course, she was right. I could drive for fun but, in the event of an emergency, I certainly wouldn't want myself behind the wheel. Our accident back in Tenterfield had proved that. I slid open the door and stepped into the rain. *Start the engine*, I said. *Just in case.*

I hated getting my hair wet. Curls would spring up all over my head, making me look Italian. I pulled the hood of my jacket up and tied it beneath my chin. Rounding the corner into Grey Street, I noticed the same dull fibro houses, overgrown yards, and toys left out in the rain. It seemed unlikely that our rich uncle had ever lived here, and I wondered if the address I'd found in the telephone book belonged to an entirely different R. Stamp, one who was poor and maybe unemployed and in no way related to me.

Number 924 was second from the end of the block. Set back from the street, the house was older than the others and made of weatherboard, painted pink. An enormous oak tree stood in the front yard with a circular seat built around it. You could notice a woman's touch: lace curtains in the window, red geraniums lining the veranda, a mossy concrete birdbath near the tree. A brick garage sat next to the house. The metal roller door was down and it rattled in the wind.

I saw no sign of my uncle or Duke, or anyone at all – no car in the drive, no lights shining from the front rooms of the house. But I did notice some footprints in the mud – pointy toes and deep heel marks that looked as if they might have been made by Duke's cowboy boots.

I crept across the lawn and down a passageway between the garage and the house. The roof guttering was overflowing, creating a waterfall between two frosted windows. I edged around it and walked further down the passage. Built on to the back of the house was what looked like a closed-in veranda, painted white. My heart leapt when I realised there was a light on inside. As I moved closer, I heard a low murmur of voices.

I hunched beneath the closed windows and tried to make out what was being said. I clearly heard a woman's laughter, the clatter of crockery. And then a more indistinct mumbling, like the people inside were speaking a secret language. I raised my head closer to the ledge, but over the drumming of the rain I still couldn't fathom what they were talking about.

And then everything bad in my life suddenly became even worse. And if I could have those moments back again – those moments from all those years ago – I certainly would have played them differently. But, then again, if I'd acted in another, more careful, way, I might not be writing this book; I wouldn't have a complete story to tell – however fragmented and confused.

Inside the house, a dog began barking. I should have run right then, but, before I disappeared, I had to know what was going on in that room. I popped my head up and peered through the window and the first thing I saw was Duke, sitting by a pot-bellied stove with a cup of tea in his hand, as if he'd lived in the house all his life. A plump, blonde woman in a floral dress was offering him a plate of biscuits. He took one and said something to her, but I still didn't understand what he was saying.

While I was gazing at the two of them, trying to figure out what was going on, I saw my father lumbering into the room on his crutches, his half-leg swaying like a clapper in a bell. His right eye was covered with a pink bandage. I went rigid for a second. Before I knew what was happening, he was staring straight back at me with his good eye, yelling, *You little bastard!* Then he grabbed the fire poker and threw it like a spear right through the windowpane.

I ducked to avoid the shattering glass and took off down the side passage. I heard footsteps running and something break inside the house. And then I glimpsed my father hobbling after me on his crutches alongside the garage. When he got to the front of it, the roller door sprang up like a stage curtain, revealing his Fairlane covered in mud. I took off across the lawn and on to the street. I heard the front door slam. I sensed someone behind me and glanced back to see Duke sprinting along about half a block away. I wasn't sure if he was after me or if he, too, was being chased by Roy. The wind and rain were driving against me as I pushed myself to run faster. By the time I'd rounded the corner into the street where Ruby was parked, Duke had almost caught up with me. We threw ourselves into the back of the van almost at the same time and yelled at her to start driving.

She hit the accelerator and made a U-turn, but, the moment we hit Grey Street again, Roy's Fairlane was behind us, about five cars away. *Christ, Mark,* yelled Ruby. *What the hell happened?*

I held the baby tight in my arms. *Ask lover boy.*

She overtook a campervan, narrowly missing an oncoming truck. We made a left, then a right. Someone honked a horn. I looked out the back window to see the Fairlane gaining on us. The van swerved, knocking me sideways, and suddenly we were flying down the New England Highway, the windscreen wipers madly slapping back and forth.

So what the hell were you doing in there? I demanded.

Nothing, said Duke in a whiny, defensive voice.

You were drinking tea and eating biscuits.

Biscuits? said Ruby. I could tell she was already pissed off with him.

Duke clasped the dashboard. *Your Uncle Bob wasn't home. His wife — your Aunty Margaret — showed me around the house. Once she realised I spoke Swedish, she made me stay and have tea.*

Let me get this straight . . . Ruby hunched over the steering wheel and passed a truck towing a horse trailer. *You put us in this spot just so you could practise your fucking Swedish?* And then she began laughing and shaking her head, as if this disaster wasn't real.

She continued to laugh as Duke gave the fogged windscreen a wipe with his hand. *I learned Swedish from a book, and from films,* he explained. *I've never been able to practise my pronunciation — your aunty's mother is from Stockholm. She insisted I stay. She was correcting my accent. I was casing the joint. Then I was checking out your father. What a whacko. He certainly freaked your aunty out when he smashed the window.*

Ruby shook her head and sighed. I peered back out the window and couldn't see the Fairlane. I figured we'd given

Roy the slip, that perhaps he couldn't drive as fast with only one leg. But, by the time we'd driven into the next town, about ten k's down the highway, I noticed the Fairlane about two blocks away, weaving crazily through the traffic, as if Roy was drunk. I could see that our father was alone, and figured that the chubby, blonde woman who was my Aunty Margaret must have stayed behind in the pink weatherboard house.

Ruby ran a red light and pushed the speedo to 110. The van shook and groaned under the strain. Rain lashed the windows and, outside, the whole world seemed to be embalmed in bad weather. I held the baby close to me as we zigzagged between lanes. Neither Duke nor I dared to say anything, in case we distracted Ruby from the road. Her eyes, reflected in the rear-view mirror, were wider than I'd ever seen them, making her look permanently startled. Road signs flashed by in a rainy blur: Llangothlin, Guyra, Black Mountain, Tilibuster. Her knuckles were white as she gripped the steering wheel.

Sometimes Roy's car disappeared from the rear-view mirror and I would pray that he'd run out of petrol. But just when I'd figure we'd given him the slip, I'd glance out the back window and see his Fairlane on the horizon, gradually gaining on us. I don't think any of us were scared about driving in daylight any more. We were travelling so fast, and through such heavy rain, that it would have been hard for a cop to spot a fourteen-year-old girl behind the wheel. Besides, we had nothing to lose now.

Armidale whizzed by in a wash of large brick houses and flooded lawns. The roads were swelling with water and barefooted kids crossed the street in yellow raincoats, carrying their shoes and socks. Rain drummed against the van and the windscreen wipers began to squeak with the extra effort. I looked behind us and realised Roy's car had disappeared from view, lost in the morning's gloomy weather. I shouted to Ruby that I couldn't see him, and was expecting her to detour down a side street or pull into a car park, but she kept to the main road. At first, I thought she was taking us further inland, towards Tamworth but, just as my heart was sinking, she steered us into a hard left and suddenly we were hurtling east towards Coffs Harbour.

My school friend Billy had once sent me a postcard from Coffs, when he was holidaying with his grandparents one Christmas. The glossy front was divided into four pictures. In three of them, the sea was so intensely blue, and the sand so golden, that they'd seemed to be coloured in by God – or so I thought at the time (I was only seven). I tried to calm myself by remembering the postcard's leaning palm trees, a woman in a bikini holding a cocktail, a blazing orange sun slipping into the ocean, even the cardboard's bevelled edges and Billy's scrawled message on the back: *I went swimming and got sunburned.* I kept the postcard for years, taped it to my bedroom wall, where I could see it as soon as I woke up in the morning. It reminded me I had things to look forward to in life, beyond my father's constant anger and the boredom of our town. Over the years, sunlight had bleached the card to a pale and faded relic of the original, and it began collecting small black specks that I later realised were bits of cockroach shit, but still I kept it on the wall until I came home one afternoon and found it gone. Roy had torn it up into strips to use as filters for his joints.

The prospect of actually seeing Coffs Harbour for myself began to excite me. My heart raced and I recalled the view of the beach and the woman in the bikini, and was embarrassed by the fact that I had a hard-on. Light-headed and dizzy, I could feel blood rushing through my veins, a throbbing in my balls. My wet armpits smelled of something deep and slightly sour. Thank God Duke and Ruby were up front, where they couldn't see me sweating and the bulge in the crotch of my jeans.

I tried to think of something else: dead babies covered in blood, dozens of them in a shallow grave — but for the first time in my life it didn't work. I thought of a man cutting off my dick, my balls, and stuffing them in my mouth, but that didn't work, either. I began counting by threes back from one hundred. I was down to sixty-nine when I glanced out the back window to see the small, pale outline of Roy's Fairlane. He was about seventy or so metres away, but I could tell he was gaining speed. I didn't know if he'd refuelled in Armidale, or if he'd solved a mechanical problem, but he seemed to be driving a lot faster.

Fuck, said Duke, glancing in the mirror. *This guy doesn't give up*. Ruby muttered something under her breath and pressed harder on the accelerator. Duke asked her if she wanted him to take over, but she either didn't hear him or thought it was a stupid question because she remained grim and silent. I thought it was kind of ironic that everything Roy had taught her about driving was now being used to defy him – to assist us in our escape – and, as she rhythmically changed gears and veered between lanes, I hoped he regretted having taught her so well.

Roy overtook a trailer and picked up speed.

He's the Terminator! said Duke. *I mean, what the fuck is his problem?*

He knows we know he killed Mum, snapped Ruby. *He wants to get us back home before we tell anyone.*

A few minutes later, Roy was right behind us – only a few car-lengths away. He was so close I could see the bandage over his eye, could almost smell his scent of stale beer and cigarettes. He was flashing his headlights, like he was some concerned stranger trying to alert us to a problem with our van. I was amazed he thought we would be so naïve as to pull over. We were nearing the crest of a rise in the road when his indicators blinked on and he swung across the double yellow lines into the lane parallel to ours, as if preparing to overtake us. But instead of slipping in front, he swerved and rammed his car against the side of the van, knocking me and the baby against the cupboards.

Fuck! cried Ruby. We briefly skidded across gravel before she turned the wheel sharply and rammed him back, knocking off his side mirror. We were almost at the crest when he swiped us again, and, for a few seconds, both vehicles seemed interlocked. I heard a thump against the side of the van as Roy tried to run us off into a paddock.

Suddenly, there was a fork in the road. Ruby veered right; Roy automatically copied her, but at that moment a car travelling in the opposite direction lurched over the rise and Roy was forced to swing a hard left. Horns honked, there was a loud squeal of tyres, and the next thing I saw was the Fairlane sailing off the side of the road and into a gully, rolling on to its side.

We all cheered and whooped. Ruby slowed down and slapped the steering wheel. Duke yelled something in Swedish. I was bouncing the baby on my knee and she was laughing as her arms fanned the air. It was at that moment I thought that maybe our mother's ghost had planted the other car there on the road, at exactly the right time, in order to protect us from our father. Or perhaps she wanted her own revenge, an attempt to take the life that had deprived her of her own. I imagined her surfing on the wind above us, arms wide, her black hair wild and wet.

Do you think he's dead? I asked.

Ruby shrugged. *Hard to say.*

Dead as a doornail, said Duke. *I saw him roll. I think his head went through the windscreen.*

That doesn't mean he's carked it, I said, although I was hoping he'd die a slow and painful death.

Just about though, said Duke. *That happened to Honey's grandfather. All his brains were splattered across the grass and these little kids playing cowboys and indians found him first and used his blood for face paint.*

Well, you couldn't do that with Roy, said Ruby. *He's got shit for brains.*

127

We were now on a much narrower bitumen road that ran beneath a canopy of trees. After a couple of minutes, we hit a muddy track that curved back and forth down the side of a mountain. Duke got the map out. We were now on a trail that threaded through Oxley Wild Rivers National Park, one that would eventually lead us to the Pacific Highway. The Pacific, I remembered, ran straight down the coast, all the way to Sydney. For the second time that day, I felt something close to happiness. In spite of being deserted at a Glen Innes motel, and the unexpected appearance of Roy, everything was sort of going to plan. Sure, we didn't get to sting Uncle Bob for some money to finance our trip, but that hadn't been part of the original plan, anyway. It was Duke who'd landed us in all that trouble, and mostly Ruby who'd pulled us out of it.

She took the turns slowly as we headed further down the mountain. The rainforest was green and wet, with kurrajongs laced with vines. On the other side of the valley, a shadowy range shone with silver streams. The rain eased to a patter. I wound down one of the windows and inhaled the delicious scent of damp earth.

When we finally reached the valley, Ruby pulled over to rest for a while. We parked by a brook that wound through an orchard. Nearby, cattle grazed and tiny calves frolicked in the water.

So, back at the house, said Ruby. *What happened?*

Duke turned and looked at me, as if I had the answer. The baby was in my arms and I put her down between two pillows.

Well, said Duke. *I did exactly what we planned. Knocked on the door. This woman opens it. I do my spiel and say my grandad built the house and ask if I can come in and look around.*

Duke shifted in his seat and unzipped his jacket.

And then? prompted Ruby.

They've got a real nice house. Lots of antiques. A chandelier. And this big grandfather clock that chimes on the hour.

I'm not talking about the fucking furniture, Duke. Ruby was getting testy and I was hoping they'd have a fight.

Well, your uncle was out getting his car fixed. Your aunty had an accent but I wasn't sure what it was. Anyway, she was real nice. It wasn't until I walked into the back room and I saw a porcelain doll holding a tiny blue and yellow flag that I realised she might come from Sweden. Once she realised I spoke the language, she insisted I stay for tea.

That doesn't mean you had to, said Ruby.

Duke began playing with the jacket of his zipper. *She corrected my pronunciation. Her accent was perfect.*

Ruby pulled a face and rolled her eyes, mimicking him in a whiny voice. *Her accent was perfect! I mean, it'd have to be fucking Swedish.* After a pause, she snapped, *Where was Roy?*

I didn't know he was there, I swear. His car wasn't out the front. It was only when I was halfway through my second cuppa that he came into the room on crutches. He'd just got up and was still wearing his pyjamas.

What did he say?

Not much. Mostly Margaret and I talked in Swedish. But when Margaret was in the bathroom, he did say one thing that was kind of weird.

Yeah? said Ruby. *What?*

Duke's face then took on a strange expression, like he didn't really want to answer the question. *Said I reminded him of his little boy, Mark.*

What's weird about that? I asked.

Duke chewed on his inside cheek and scratched his head. *He told me his son was dead.*

Dead? I repeated, hardly believing what I was hearing. If it was Duke's idea of a joke it wasn't very funny.

A shark took him at a beach one day, Duke continued. *And Roy told me that's how he lost his leg, trying to save his son from a Great White.*

I didn't want to believe Duke, but I had to admit it was such an outlandish story that it seemed entirely plausible my father would say such a thing. The thought of him spreading rumours that I was dead unnerved me, as if it wasn't so much a lie as a chilling premonition.

I suddenly felt as if I was suffocating, as if the stench of the van was trapped in my lungs. I opened the side door and crawled outside. It was still drizzling but I didn't care any more. The ranges had turned blue with rain. The air was fresh and pungent. I kneeled down and dipped my face into the stream, allowing the currents to run across my skin like thin, icy fingers. Occasionally, I parted my lips and swallowed a mouthful of water. It was so cold it made me feel alive or, rather, it reminded me I was still alive and not inside the belly of a Great White or, worse, reduced to a knob of shark shit floating through the ocean. I don't know how long I crouched there, with my face submerged, but after a while, I felt someone pulling at my collar.

Ruby dragged me from the stream. *What are you trying to do, Mark?* she demanded. *Bloody kill yourself?*

The wind stung my wet face and neck, but I didn't mind. Again, it dispelled that dead feeling inside me. While I felt pain, I was still here on earth, and not in the afterlife with my mother.

Ruby walked me back to the van and dried me off. We sat inside and Duke passed around a block of Club chocolate. He tried to cheer us up by telling a story about what he and Honey would do to cadge free restaurant meals. Honey always carried a large, dead cockroach around in a matchbox and, after half-eating her steak or whatever, she'd slip it onto her plate and scream. They'd always receive a grovelling apology from the manager, an entirely new meal, and would never have to part with a cent.

That sounds cool, said Ruby, impressed. *We'll have to do that, the first town we hit.* She licked some chocolate from her fingers. *Hey, Duke,* she added, *whatever happened to Honey?*

He shrugged and gazed through the windscreen.

Ruby nudged his shoulder. *Something must've happened.*

Not really, he murmured, shifting in his seat.

Maybe she's dead, I said. I don't know why I blurted that out. It was just the first thing that popped into my mind.

Look, said Duke. *She ran off with some other guy, OK?*

Yeah? asked Ruby. *Who?*

Duke sighed. I could tell he didn't like talking about it. *I don't know. Just some guy she met on the road. He had a car. I didn't. She likes guys with cars. Especially late-model ones.*

I sensed Ruby was curious to hear more but, as far as Duke was concerned, the subject was closed. Still, I couldn't resist taunting him a bit, especially after the way he'd treated me the night before.

Did you love her? I asked, in my most serious, innocent voice.

He bristled and then – I guess for something to do – he wound down the window. He stuck his hand outside, palm-up, as if he was trying to catch fresh rainwater.

Did you? echoed Ruby, a little more sharply.

He rubbed his face with his wet hand and slicked back his hair. *I don't know,* he said. *What's love, anyway? She was just a good root, that's all.*

Ruby's eyes narrowed and she pursed her lips. I could tell she was mentally comparing herself and her sexual techniques with this girl she'd never met. It was then that I felt sorry for my sister. She could handle a four-wheel-drive, stand up to our father, destroy telephone boxes, and shoot wild pigs, but, when it came to boys, she was as vulnerable as a baby.

I think I was still shaken by the car chase with Roy, because I began to suspect that he wasn't seriously injured. It was just a feeling I had, like sensing a storm a long time before it actually begins to thunder. My temples ached and my neck grew tight. I looked out the window and expected to see his dented Fairlane careening down the trail behind us, blood on his face, eyes blazing.

C'mon, I said. *Let's get going. This place is giving me the creeps.*

Duke and Ruby traded seats and he took over the driving. It was easy to see their moods had changed. Both were quiet and sullen. I could tell Ruby was still stewing over Honey, and so was Duke, but of course for different reasons. I, myself, didn't go in for all that lovey-dovey stuff. Just witnessing what it had done to my mother and father had convinced me that romance was a dirty trick. All that agony for so little joy. I'd already decided, a few years before, that I would never marry or get a girl pregnant because it was possible she could give birth to a little Roy and my adult life would end up being as painful as my childhood. I wanted to make movies or be a writer. Then the whole world would love me – or so I thought at the time. I was only twelve years old and had romantic notions of what it would be like to be an artist. (I enjoy writing but it doesn't pay the rent, and all my friends think I'm a wanker because I haven't had anything published yet – unless you count a few film and CD reviews for the local street press.)

The logging track wove through a mossy rainforest. The eucalypts and cypress pines were high and green. Every now and then, I glimpsed a flash of wattle blossoms pressing through the foliage. On the other side of the gorge, a waterfall unravelled like a bright, metallic ribbon. It was one of the most beautiful places I'd ever seen, except on television, of course. So different from the granite boulders and weedy paddocks of the town where we came from.

The baby woke and I fed her some chocolate. We were down to our last nappy and, even though we'd bathed her that morning, she was already starting to stink. I was beginning to regret having returned the Huggies in exchange for Duke's twelve bucks. When I changed her, I had to improvise with one of my T-shirts and the blue gaffer tape. She looked like a miniature Egyptian mummy, but, as usual, she didn't seem to mind.

Ruby was exhausted. She crawled into the back and curled up on the mattress, so the baby and I sat up front with Duke. The track was muddy and he drove a little slower than I would have preferred. I was impatient to get as far away from my father as possible and closer to the sea.

Can't we go a little faster? I asked.

Duke slowed down even more. *What's the hurry?*

I didn't want to annoy him, but I didn't believe his story about Roy being dead. *The baby needs some nappies*, I said. *And I'm really hungry.*

We haven't got any money.

I'll nick 'em.

There's a town coming up soon, said Duke. *It's called Bellbird or Bellbrook or something.* He changed gears but didn't speed up and I knew he was doing it deliberately to annoy me.

Did you and Honey go to that town? I asked. *Did you root her there? Is that where she ran off with the guy who owned a car?*

I saw it on the map, smartarse. It might have been my

imagination but I was sure he pressed a little harder on the accelerator. Now I'd found his weak spot, I intended to keep prodding it.

The town was so small, it only had one shop and a pub. Duke pulled up about a block away from the centre but kept the motor running. I left the baby on my seat and dashed into the general store. There was one woman at the counter near the door and another at a sandwich bar down the back. No matter how many times I roamed up and down the aisles, I couldn't find an angle that would conceal me from them and allow me to steal some food. Finally, I picked some disposable nappies off a shelf and ordered three pies from the sandwich lady.

I was prepared to spend Duke's twenty bucks because I didn't want to waste any more time. I placed the items on the counter. The cashier was on the phone, giving instructions to someone about how to make gravy. Just after she said the words 'Three tablespoons of stock', I heard the horn of our van honking. I looked through the window and saw that Duke had pulled up directly in front of the shop. I swiped up the pies and nappies and bolted out the door. The women shouted after me, but I kept running down the stairs and flung myself into the van. Duke took off before I could pick up the baby and she fell on to the floor and began howling.

What the hell? I said, picking her up. She'd hit her head and already her forehead was beginning to swell.

Roy, yelled Ruby, staring out the back window. *Down in the valley. About a k-and-a-half away.*

The baby's tears were hot against my fingers. As we picked up speed, I noticed the speedometer edge from seventy to seventy-five to eighty … Duke's face had contracted into a furrow of concentration as he changed gears and took hard curves. Cattle rushed past and, all of a sudden, the countryside that had, only minutes before, seemed so tranquil and serene was now bleak and ugly. Heavy wind rattled the van and the constant rain threatened to run us off the road.

You said he went through the windscreen, I muttered, but Duke either didn't hear me or chose not to respond. I was angry at him for having taken his time earlier. People always talk about the dangers of speeding; no one ever mentions the risks of moving too slowly through life.

The road was slippery and sometimes we found ourselves skidding dangerously close to the edge of a precipice that dropped into a rocky valley. At one point, Duke swung the van so sharply that one of the back wheels momentarily spun off the edge. Ruby yelled, *You said you could fucking drive, moron!* The baby was still crying and rubbing at her eyes. I tried to calm her down by bobbing her on my knee and quietly singing, 'Oranges and Lemons', her favourite song. Usually she laughed and clapped her hands when she heard it, but, the more I sang, the louder she howled, as if the melody was torturing her. *For Christsakes, Mark!* yelled Ruby. *Shut her up, will you?* I held her to the window, blew raspberries on her belly, tickled her neck. Finally, I fed her half of one of the cold pies. Her face was now red, a big bruise rising above her right eye, but, after she finished eating, she finally settled down in my arms.

If a car appeared in front of us, Duke now didn't hesitate to overtake it, even if the visibility was bad. Ruby continued to keep a lookout for Roy. Occasionally, she'd announce that she could see his car in the distance, on the crest of a hill, or rounding a bend. I could hear her muttering, *Fuck, fuck*, to herself as she kept her vigil, like some religious fanatic chanting a pornographic mantra.

By the time we were hurtling down the side of a mountain not far from Kempsey, she hadn't spotted him for quite a while, probably at least ten minutes. We all hoped that he'd run out of petrol, or had had another crash. For a few moments, there seemed a real possibility that we'd given him the slip.

As we neared the floor of the valley, however, we saw three cars sitting in the middle of the road, each behind the other, like some stalled gypsy caravan. At first we thought it might be another police roadblock, or some other authority who'd been ordered to track us down. Duke slowed a little and peered warily through the windscreen. The three cars were white, but different models and years. As we got closer, I saw two kids in the back of the third one, punching each other, and a man standing outside, holding a golf umbrella, and then it became obvious why they'd all stopped so suddenly in the one place: swelling with rain, the nearby river had burst its banks and had completely flooded the trail.

Ruby cursed and leapt from the side door. I sat the baby in my seat and jumped out after her. We ran past the man with the umbrella to the water's edge. The flooded river was pockmarked with the heavy rain. It cascaded across our path in fast, heavy currents. It was hard to tell how deep it was, but its width was about the size of two tennis courts. A tree had fallen on one of the banks, its upper branches pointing at the clouds like thin, gnarled fingers.

Before I could stop her, Ruby was wading into the water, not even bothering to roll up her jeans. *Hey*, I called. *What are you doing?*

She didn't answer, just pushed against the current as it rose around her knees, thighs, hips. The water was the colour of rusty nails. By the time she reached the middle of the flood, it was surging around her waist. From where I stood, she looked impossibly small and vulnerable, as if she was deliberately tempting the river to sweep her away. Then she looked up at the sky for what seemed a long time, but was probably only a few moments. If I didn't know her better, I would have said that she was praying to God or maybe the ghost of our mother as to what the fuck she was supposed to do next.

She wiped the wet hair away from her face and rested her palms face-down on the corrugated surface of the water, like a medium placing her hands on a séance table. I heard the man with the umbrella, who was still behind me, remark in an American accent, *You know, it's not safe out there.* And then Ruby suddenly turned around – her eyes wide with panic – and began hurrying back towards the shore, her arms stroking through the water like frantic oars. I could see she was trembling from the cold and her face had turned blue. As she waded from the flood, I noticed she'd lost one shoe and her jeans were patterned with mud and bracken.

She ran straight past me, as if I wasn't there. The American asked loudly, *So where are your parents?* He was a short man who was further dwarfed by his enormous yellow umbrella. I ignored him and shot off after Ruby.

By the time I'd caught up with her, she'd opened the door on the driver's side and was dragging Duke out of the van. *Jesus, what the hell?* he yelled, trying to wrestle himself back inside. The people in the other cars were popping their heads out of windows, wondering what was going on. Ruby slapped Duke hard on the face. *Just shut up and get in the back!* she barked, giving him one final yank. He staggered for a moment and fell to his knees in the mud, still holding his sore right cheek. I didn't want to mess with her when she was in this kind of mood. I just scrambled back into the passenger seat and held the baby close, preparing myself for whatever it was that Ruby had planned for us. I figured the safest thing to do would be to back up and try to find a side trail.

By the time Duke had crawled into the back, Ruby had turned on the ignition and was revving up the engine. *I saw him when I was out there,* she said, nodding at the flood. *Less than a k away.* I wasn't sure if she'd actually spotted him, or whether she'd had some sort of supernatural vision.

And then she did something that to this day still seems incredible to me. She pushed down on the accelerator and headed straight for the flood waters, as if she'd rather we all drown together than be returned to live with our father.

The American was at the water's edge, still clutching his umbrella, and, when he realised what Ruby was about to attempt, he spread his legs and waved his free arm, trying to block our way. It was a stupid thing for him to do because I knew even then that no one person or thing could stop her now, and she sped straight towards him like he was a human target begging to be mown down. I heard him cry out as he stumbled sideways, just as we were about to hit him. He fell into the water and his upturned umbrella was whisked away by the currents.

Ruby slowed down as she steered us further into the flood. I could feel the pull of the water dragging us to the left. Even Duke went silent as he stuck his head between the two front seats. I heard the American calling to us, as if from the end of a very long tunnel. I glanced back and could see several adults and a couple of kids now standing at the shore, waving at us to come back. The rain continued to fall. The water-level rose around us and began seeping into the van, washing over my feet and ankles. I wound the window all the way up and hugged the baby closer. Ruby continued to steer us forward with a grim desperation. The river was now swirling around us, carrying branches, ferns, feathers. Everything smelled dank and loamy, as if each decomposing thing in the river had been churned up by the flood. By this time, the water inside the van had risen to my knees and the baby, intrigued, was leaning over and raking her fingers through it. I could hear floating objects in the back of the van bumping against the built-in cupboard.

We'd just reached the halfway mark, around the spot where Ruby had been standing, when, for the first time, I thought we could actually make it to the other side. The water was now lapping around the front seats and I had to stand the baby on my lap. The corpse of a calf floated by, its shiny black eyes wide and startled, as if it couldn't believe it was no longer alive. And, as I watched it being swept away, the van suddenly stalled and the wheels began spinning in the mud.

Shit! cried Ruby, punching the steering wheel. The river continued to push and eddy around us, splashing against the windows. Branches bumped and scraped against the side. I wondered if Duke could swim and if we should try to save anything. And then I glanced in the rear-view mirror, hoping that the American was still on the shore and would be prepared to wade through to help us. Not only did I see him, pinch-faced and leaning on the bonnet of his car, soaking wet, but I also glimpsed a flash of red through the bush, and then saw Roy's Fairlane heading down the mountain trail.

Ruby must have seen him at almost the same time, because she yelled to me and Duke, *For fuck's sake, get out! Get out and push!*

Sinking myself into that flood was the last thing I wanted to do, but Ruby kept screaming at us. The baby began crying, writhing in my arms, slippery as a dying fish. Ruby lunged across and flipped the handle on my door. Suddenly, the river rushed into the van and the baby, still writhing, was no longer in my arms, but was being swept away, howling, her tiny fists punching the air.

Ruby cried out as I leapt into the flood after the baby. The currents were carrying my little sister off in the same direction as the calf, towards a cluster of gaunt willows straining against the flood. I saw her roll a couple of times. The thick mud seemed to suck down my every step, as if I was struggling through quicksand. I kicked off my shoes, stretched out my arms, and threw myself into the river, allowing it to take me. I could still hear the baby howling as the flood rushed me forward like a piece of driftwood. I stroked my arms and kicked, striving to move faster, but became entangled in the branches of a fallen tree. As I writhed and twisted I could still hear Ruby yelling, and glimpsed Roy's car, now about a quarter of the way down the mountain. The water was loud in my ears. I freed myself and continued to paddle frantically downstream but, as I scanned the surface of the water, I could no longer see the baby. There were the willows, the protruding rocks, the muddy trail that rose from the other side of the flood, but no little sister. Panicking, I glanced all around me. The red-and-white Fairlane was growing larger as it took a curve of the mountain. I hurried forward, to the last spot I thought I'd seen her. Suddenly, a strong current dragged me down and I found myself struggling for air. I kicked and stroked against its pull. The flood was now the colour of dark tobacco and it was only then that I registered how cold I was. I thought my lungs would burst and I would drown right then – that this would be my watery grave.

When I finally surfaced, gasping, I found myself beneath the hanging fronds of one of the willows. As I sucked in as much air as I could, I saw something out of the corner of my eye, only a couple of metres away. The baby was wedged into the bough of the tree, her arms around a branch, as if she were clinging to her mother.

She wasn't making any sound at all – not even a gurgle. But, when I finally got to her, I was relieved to see the rise and fall of her chest. She was shivering with cold. Her wet hair was pasted against her cheeks and her face was scratched and bleeding. I gathered her in my arms and pressed her to me.

I began the struggle back to the van. As I pressed against the currents, I could see Roy's car was about halfway down the mountain, in front of a big truck. The American was sitting on his bonnet, arms folded, watching us, as if we were some kind of nightclub act. The baby hugged me around the neck, shivering, while I took long steps through the thick mud. I found I could move faster if I turned and walked backwards, so that's what I did, buffeting the baby against the surge of water.

When I finally reached the open door of the van, I passed her through to Ruby. *Thank God!* she cried. *Is she breathing? Is she OK?* She was drying the baby's face with the sleeve of her jacket. I began climbing back into the van. *No!* she barked, looking in the rear-view mirror. *Hurry up and push!*

I wiped my eyes with the back of my hand and caught my breath momentarily. I was exhausted and cold and wanted to collapse, but I did as I was told and waded around to the back of the van, where I found a naked Duke casually leaning against the window, like he was standing in a friend's backyard swimming pool. His skin was as white as my underarms.

Ruby flicked on the ignition and tried to rev the engine while Duke and I threw our weight against the rear. I could hear the wheels spinning and groaning in the mud before the engine spluttered and died. While she tried to start it up again, I looked over my shoulder to see Roy almost at the bottom of the mountain now. His car had been damaged in the accident – the windscreen was cracked, one headlight was smashed, and the entire left side was badly dented, but it hadn't seemed to slow him down too much.

I heard the engine cough, Duke and I pushed hard, our feet sinking into the mud. As Ruby revved, we finally managed to dislodge the van from the river bed. We pushed it about seven or eight metres, where the water-level was lower, but the engine choked and died again. Through the window, I could see the baby was sitting on Ruby's lap and, for a moment, it seemed as if she was the one driving. I glanced back to see Roy pulling up by the river's edge, right beside the American. *Hurry!* I bawled to Ruby. *C'mon! He's here!* His side door opened. I saw a flash of one of his crutches and then out swung his good leg.

The engine murmured and spluttered again. I was pushing so hard I thought my guts would burst, that my muscles would snap like guitar strings. Duke was growling and groaning under the strain. The wheels whirred and spun in the mud. I could hear the horn of Roy's car blaring, like some enormous prehistoric bird. Suddenly the engine hiccuped and, right when I thought I could push no more, the van jolted forward and began moving through the water. Duke and I grinned at each other and continued to push, while Roy's horn kept sounding, over and over.

The van finally lurched onto the opposite bank. The river began pouring out of it like water streaming through a colander. Ruby stopped for a moment and Duke and I jumped back in. The baby was covered with mud and lichen; the seats were soaked; the air smelled of mould, but at least we were all still alive. The engine groaned as we headed up the track. Before we rounded a curve, I glanced back to see Roy's Fairlane driving into the flood. The American was still sitting on the bonnet of his car, watching and shaking his head.

I didn't like to think about how much time we had before our father caught up with us again. Maybe he'd get bogged, as we had. Maybe he'd clamber out of the car and the river would swallow him. He used to be a strong swimmer, but, now that his right leg was gone, he never went near the water.

The baby was trembling in my arms, so I towelled her down with one of Duke's T-shirts and wrapped her in the dry half of his sleeping bag. While I'd been trying to save her, Duke had sensibly removed his leather jacket, shirt and trousers, and had stored them in the van's highest cupboard, and now he was casually putting them back on, as if this sort of catastrophe happened to him every day. Most of my other clothes were wet and I was forced to change into one of Ruby's tops and a pair of her corduroy jeans, which were a size too big. This made me think of our mother, and how weird it was that she'd been wearing my sister's clothes the day that Roy had killed her. Or maybe he'd murdered her first and then dressed her in the top and mini-skirt. Still, it didn't make sense to me – none of it did. All the while, we kept looking back but saw no other cars on the trail.

It finally stopped raining. The clouds thinned and parted, and, for the first time that day, I glimpsed a sliver of blue sky. My stomach settled and I realised I was hungry. The bush soon faded into fenced paddocks and hobby farms. The trail ended and Ruby swung us on to a bitumen road, where we could pick up speed. Houses began appearing, only a few at first, and then lawns with plaster garden gnomes and miniature windmills.

It was late afternoon by the time we drove into Kempsey. The main street was wide, with cars parked parallel on either side. We passed a cop shop and Ruby, obviously relieved to have escaped our father again, without any help from the police, stuck her head out the window and poked the air with her middle finger, though there was no one on the steps to see it.

Up ahead, however, was a railway track with two lanes of cars banked up before it. The boom gates were down. Ruby sighed with frustration and muttered to herself. As we drew closer, a freight train began roaring through town. We slowed down and joined one line of the vehicles. To calm myself, I began counting the carriages, as if my calculations could lessen how many there were, or at least speed up the train. At number nine, Ruby coughed and spat on the road; at eleven, she hissed, *Shit, shit, shit.* At thirteen, she yelled,

What is this? Fucking Noah's Ark? I agreed with her: it seemed impossible that a single engine could carry such a long and heavy load.

Duke piped up, *Let me take over. You come back here and have a rest.* For once, I thought Duke had a good idea and I even agreed with him. By the thirty-third carriage, they'd swapped places. At long last, the final carriage – number thirty-six – swept past. The boom gates slowly rose and the traffic began to flow.

As we bumped over the railway lines, however, I looked out the window and was sure I could see Roy's Fairlane in the distance, covered in mud, about half a k away. I didn't say anything, but I could tell by the deep frown on Duke's face that he had glimpsed it too.

A long iron bridge appeared before us. Duke overtook a car and then we were speeding above a wide, copper-coloured river. The sun came out and I squinted as the van filled with glare. We swerved on to the Pacific Highway, heading south. I assumed we'd stay on the main route and allow it to take us to Sydney, to our aunt, but, after five or so minutes, Ruby yelled, *Get in the left lane. We're going bush.* Duke slowed down and did as he was told. He turned left off the highway and within moments we were driving down a narrow, sealed road, heading for a place called Crescent Head. I looked up at the sky and saw the remaining clouds parting like celestial gates. The winding road was lined with tall gums and ferns, tiny white flowers amid clumps of clover. Ruby kept a lookout from the back and announced every so often that the coast was clear – that she couldn't see Roy's car behind us. The baby had perked up and, in spite of her bruises, she began banging her left hand on the side of the dashboard. I wound the window down and thought I could smell salt on the breeze.

The town came upon us sooner than I expected: large, double-storey houses dotting the side of a hill. And then I caught my first glimpse of the ocean, a triangle of shimmering green between two rises of land. We rounded a curve and the beach suddenly appeared before me: a long stretch of eggshell-white sand fringed with grass and trees. Waves rose and folded into themselves, rushing towards the shore. Seagulls arced in the air. I thought I'd seen beauty earlier in the national park but nothing could compare with my first sighting of the sea.

Duke pulled up in the car park. *That showed him!* he boasted. We all climbed out of the van and the ocean breeze ruffled my hair. Ruby shaded her eyes and squinted into the distance, making sure Roy wasn't on the road behind us. When she was satisfied we'd given him the slip, she grabbed a dry bedsheet and we walked down a path to the beach. I was stunned by how big it was, a huge half-moon of water curving into the horizon, so wide and endless it made me feel as if the rest of my life could be just as infinite, as if I could do anything.

Duke ran ahead, somersaulting onto the sand. He began walking on his hands and singing something in Swedish. Ruby unfurled the sheet near a rock shaped like an artichoke. I was surprised by how warm it was, considering it was winter. There was a group of surfers further down, some not even wearing wetsuits. Clouds bobbed across the horizon, like tiny grey boats.

Duke walked towards us on his hands and Ruby pushed him over. He jumped up and tackled her, and they began wrestling each other. Ruby was squealing and punching as they tussled back and forth. I put the baby down and took off the top I'd borrowed from Ruby, welcoming the sun on my back. The relief of having escaped Roy yet again was beginning to fill me, like dawn light in a room. I pressed my dirty feet into the sand and squeezed its soft, powdery grain between my toes. It was strangely comforting, so different from the oily mud of our town swimming hole.

Ruby and Duke began pulling each other's clothes off as they rolled back and forth. Her jumper came off, then her T-shirt, while she managed to unbuckle his belt and reef his jeans halfway down his legs. Next came her jeans, his jacket. It was like some mad game of strip poker without cards. Once Ruby was down to her black bra and panties, she squealed again, scampered on all fours across the sand, and struggled to her feet. They were obviously crazy and giddy with relief. Duke pulled his windcheater off and chased her down to the water. She ran into the breakers and Duke tackled her again. The wind carried their laughter across the sand.

I knew we were almost out of petrol and didn't like the idea of siphoning more fuel to get us to Sydney. Maybe we could dump the van and Duke could steal a car, especially since he was always skiting about how many times he'd done it. Ruby's jumper began to blow away and I leapt up and caught it. Then I gathered all the rest of their clothes and put them in a pile on a corner of the sheet.

It was when I dropped Duke's leather jacket that I noticed the silver handle of his pistol sticking out of the inside pocket. I reached over to grab it and, as I did so, his invitation to the Swedish Consulate and some other things fell out. A laminated fake ID, stating that Duke was three years older than he'd told us, with a picture of him grinning stupidly at the camera; a small, smooth gemstone that I recognised as a rose quartz; and a colour photograph of Duke, probably taken when he was about eleven, with a tall woman in her early forties, who was wearing an orange bikini. She had the same dark, curly hair as Duke, the same amber irises and white, untanned skin. They were arm-in-arm and were looking into each other's eyes. In her free hand, she held an unlit cigarette.

I turned the photo over and was surprised to see, printed in blue biro, *Honey and me, Sawtell Beach*. I flipped it back and gazed at the woman again – with her crow's feet and wrinkled brow she was definitely past forty, though still quite pretty. Duke was gazing up at her, head cocked, lips slightly pursed, as if preparing for a kiss.

I glanced up to see Ruby running from the shallow breakers, breasts jiggling in her wet black bra. I shoved the photo back into the inside pocket, along with the gun and everything else. By the time she'd run across the sand, I was sitting back, pretending to teach the baby to talk.

Why don't you go in? she asked, as she stood dripping above me and shaking her wet hair. *I'll keep an eye on her.*

I said nothing about the photo, just jumped to my feet and peeled off my jeans. As I walked towards the shore, my skin prickled with goosebumps. The sun was setting behind me, making my shadow loom large across the sand. I saw Duke duck below the surface of the water and stand on his hands, so all I could see of him were two small white feet waving in the air. I now felt that something had forever changed between us, that he could no longer hurt or taunt me.

The water swept towards me, foaming around my feet, my ankles, cold and almost ticklish. I had waited for this moment – to see the ocean – all my life, and, now that it was happening, I felt dizzy and light-headed. I walked further into the sea as the breakers rose and bubbled, splashing me in the face, the tang of salt water on my tongue. I raised my arms and submerged my head. A current of warmer water enveloped my limbs and I could feel the silt and mud of the flood washing away.

When I came up for air, I found myself rising on the same wave as Duke. We were both facing the horizon, where sunlight glanced off the surface of the ocean in hundreds of tiny stars. The wave passed and I felt my feet touch the sandy bed of the sea.

Don't drown, little boy, said Duke. *We still need someone to change the nappies.*

I swam closer to him, so he could hear me clearly. *Hey Duke*, I said, treading water. *Did Honey change your nappies?*

I could already see the shock in his face, as if he'd seen a shark.

Did she wipe your arse? I added.

He frowned and splashed water in my face. *What the fuck are you talking about?*

Did she carry you on her hip? Did she smack you on the arse? Did you suck all the milk from her tits?

He rushed at me, hands clawing the surface of the water. I waded backwards, just out of his reach. *You've never had a girlfriend in your life,* I said. *Wait till I tell Ruby she fucked a virgin.*

His hands were suddenly around my neck. I kicked and flailed, trying to escape his grip. We rose and dropped on another wave. He pushed me underwater and held me down and, as I struggled to free myself, I accidentally took several gulps of salt water. I grabbed Duke's balls and squeezed them so tight that, even from under the water, I could hear him screaming.

He released his hold and I came up for air. *You fucking cocksucker!* he yelled, as I coughed and spluttered. *You think you know everything, don't you?*

He was treading water and looked as if he was holding his wounded balls with one hand. *Well, you wanna know the real reason your father lost his leg?*

I swam a few metres backwards. *You don't know shit, Duke.*

He waded towards me, a queer, knowing smile on his face.

It was Ruby, he said in a low voice.

I rolled my eyes and laughed.

Your dad has a shed, doesn't he? He was passed out inside it one night.

It was one of the most outlandish stories I'd ever heard. *That's crap, Duke. Ruby was closer to Roy than any of us.*

He swam up close and grabbed me by the hair. *Oh yeah. They were close, all right.*

Then he let go and shoved me away. My limbs felt weightless, as if I'd forgotten how to swim. I sank into the water and came up again. I was convinced that Duke was just messing with my head, that he was taking revenge for what I now knew about Honey. *You don't know shit, Duke. Ruby would've told me.*

Duke smirked and threw a piece of seaweed in my face. I peeled it off and floated over a rising swell. Suddenly, the water seemed to drop in temperature and I found myself shivering. More seaweed surrounded me, rubbery tendrils curling around my limbs. I imagined something as creepy as the Loch Ness monster preparing to pull me into the ocean's depths, and this dread sent me splashing and kicking towards the shore. A large wave rose and carried me for a few seconds before breaking so roughly it shoved me down and I rolled and rolled against the sea floor, my mouth and nose filling with sand. I thought I would never surface, that I would drown right then and there, and my father's story about my being eaten by a shark would be proven true. I could feel the scratch of shells against my skin, the jagged points of rocks, a tangle of seaweed at my ankles.

The wave finally released me, not far from the shore. I stood on my knees, gasping for air and wiping the wet sand from my face. When I could breathe properly again, I scrambled to my feet and staggered up the beach. A cold breeze hit me and made me shiver. Even from a distance, I could see that Ruby had dried herself and put her clothes back on. She was sitting on the sheet, eating one of the cold pies. The baby was playing in the sand. The sun had fallen behind the trees and the sky was the reddish colour of autumn leaves. It was all beginning to make sense to me now, why our mother's corpse had been dressed in Ruby's clothes.

Ruby glanced at my hair, which was still matted with wet sand. *What happened to you?*

I picked up Duke's leather jacket, pulled the pistol from his pocket and aimed it directly at her head.

Stop mucking around, Mark . . . she said.

In the distance, on the beach path, I glimpsed a figure silhouetted against the sky, as small and narrow as my finger.

Is it true? I demanded, still aiming the gun between Ruby's eyes.

She looked genuinely perplexed, like she had no idea what I was talking about. *What the fuck are you doing, Mark?*

The figure was now hobbling down the path towards the sand, about forty metres away.

How did you do it? I said, trying to steady my trembling hand. *An axe?*

Ruby edged back, trying to avoid the barrel of the gun, but my aim followed her. The blood drained from her face. *What do you mean?* she asked, hugging her knees tighter.

I flipped the safety catch and took a step closer. *Don't fuck with me, Ruby.*

At that, her eyes welled with tears and she began hyperventilating. The figure behind her was growing bigger as it struggled across the sand.

I wanted to tell you, she said breathlessly, *so many times*. She pressed her face into her hands, like a little kid watching the goriest bit of a horror movie. *He fucked me so often I couldn't help falling pregnant*. She touched the head of the baby, as if she were blessing her. *Anyway, he got what he deserved*, she added, starting to hiccup. *Why do you think he sold his power saw?*

I glanced at the baby pushing her fingers through the sand, and tried to contemplate the idea that she had come out of Ruby, that this girl was not only my half-sister but also my niece. It seemed incredible, impossible, but the more I gazed at her button nose and prominent chin, her red curls and deep green eyes, the more she seemed like Ruby.

Sometimes I love her, she murmured, *sometimes I hate her*.

My hands were still shaking but I raised the pistol and aimed. He was almost upon us now, his crutches arcing back and forth in a whirl of flying sand. Ruby turned around and, when she saw him, snatched up the baby and cowered behind me. I could see his bandages, his straggly beard dotted with crumbs, his lips that folded inwards, like the women's cunts I'd seen in porn magazines, because he'd lost his dentures again. I imagined him raping my sister, over and over, and the various ways he might have killed our mother. I saw her suffocating beneath a pillow, being stabbed in the heart, poisoned with her morning cup of tea. Roy opened his mouth to say something but, before he could get the words out, my hand tightened around the pistol, my finger squeezed hard on the trigger, and a shot exploded. As he fell backwards, blood fanned across the sand, and seagulls squawked and scattered into the sunset. People further down the beach yelled and began running towards us. And, right then, the baby grinned, raised her hand and began laughing, laughing hysterically, as if she was being tickled. I looked up to where she was pointing and saw the first of the night's pale stars pressing through the clouds.

7

After months of rumour and gossip, the town and I finally knew the truth about how Roy lost his leg. Of course, all this happened years ago and most of the people in this story have gone their separate ways. But, at the time, news of our parents' murders was flashed around the globe, even on American TV. A boy in Russia read about me in the paper and wrote me an admiring letter. Apparently, he performed a copycat murder. He shot his own father and cut off his leg, which wasn't exactly what I did, but the kid did seem pretty confused at the time. He signed off by thanking me, by saying everyone in Russia would forever know his name.

Even now, from what I hear, no one sits on Roy's stool at the pub – it's like a kind of creepy electric chair that everyone keeps their distance from. But teenage girls, probably overcome by morbid fascination, still vie for the school desk that I carved my name in when I was twelve. And I'm told they all congregate down behind the old gym, where our mother fell pregnant with Ruby. People in town still drive past our old house and point out the shed where I found the corpse.

Our parents were buried in separate graves in the Glen Innes Cemetery. Within days, Roy's headstone was covered in graffiti and his plot was littered with empty beer bottles. As a matter of fact, the cemetery isn't far from where Ruby, the baby and I ended up living. After the police inquiry and the court hearing, our Uncle Bob and Aunty Margaret took us in, since they have no kids of their own. It was a relief to live a kind of normal life after everything we'd endured but Ruby and I both ended up on Prozac. She's still on a high dosage – 150 mg a day. Me, I'm down to seventy-five

The baby, whom Ruby ended up calling Sapphire, after our mother, grew up mildly autistic and still lives with Bob and Margaret. She's heading into her teens now and Aunty Margaret is probably teaching her conversational Swedish.

After the news hit the press, the Swedish Consulate contacted Duke through the police, and invited him to a private lunch in Melbourne, where he finally got to meet the King and Queen of Sweden, which was even better than meeting them at a Gala Reception. We all saw his picture in the paper, standing between Carl Gustaf and Silvia, grinning broadly, his borrowed tuxedo too big for him. Duke hadn't seen his own mother, Honey, in over two years, but when the authorities contacted her in Darwin, where she was living with a pawnbroker, they forced her to take him back. The last we heard, he was juggling and tightrope-walking on the streets of Paris and making a tidy fortune.

When Ruby left home at eighteen, she began living with a motor mechanic. She gave birth again, to a set of twins, and moved to a housing estate near Lismore. We talk on the phone a couple of times a month, but we never discuss what happened that week we were on the run. She's now blonde and twenty-five and wants to go to TAFE to study relationship counselling.

Even after his death, my father was still wrecking people's lives. After I shot Roy, Sparrow Turner, from Walgett Trucking, ended up getting back together with his former fiancée, Tanya, and marrying her in the Tenterfield Catholic Church. They even managed to get her kids back from foster care. But she and her eldest, Halo, never made up. Tanya apparently had her committed to a Brisbane psychiatric hospital, where I believe she still lives.

Upon hearing of Roy's death, Clare Wilcott, Roy's former young teacher at the high school, fled the town and her marriage and ended up here in Sydney, hooked on crystal meth. I used to see her on Darlinghurst Road, lifting up her skirt and yelling at men to come and fuck her.

Me, I'm unmarried and now live in Kings Cross, around the corner from my Aunty Candy, who is finally off smack and in a methadone program. At dusk, I sit on my balcony and gaze up at the sky, still wondering how we survived, waiting for darkness and the night's one thousand eyes.

Acknowledgments

Thanks to Nerida Silva for teaching me how to camp illegally and how to survive in the bush.

Thanks to Matt Manex and Lloyd Tepper for demonstrating their petrol-stealing skills.